AN UNEXPECTED FAMILY
Orphan Train Romance Series, Book 1

Written by Zoe Matthews

Preface

Between 1850 and 1930, around 250,000 abandoned and orphaned children traveled on trains from the east coast of United States to different towns in the west in hopes of finding new homes. Most came from New York City.

This plan was started by a man named Charles Loring Brace who was very concerned about the number of young children living on the streets of New York. He worked with an orphanage named "Children's Aid Society." He came up with this idea that, if these children were taken west and placed in homes in rural communities, they would have a chance for a better life rather than spending their childhood in an orphanage or on the streets. Forty-five states eventually participated in this program, including the countries of Mexico and Canada.

Posters were placed around towns to advertise "Homes Wanted for Orphans." There usually was a committee in the town that would screen interested parents and help place the orphans. These children were supposed to be adopted and treated as family members. This wasn't always the case though, and sometimes children were placed in bad situations.

Despite this loosely structured plan, many children did find loving homes with caring parents and families.

Chapter 1

AMANDA DRAKE WALKED into the general store and headed to the back of the large room. She was looking for some specific fabric for a new order she had received for a morning dress from the mayor's wife, Mrs. Margaret Porter. She had asked for green-plaid fabric, buttons, lace and ribbon. Amanda was hoping she would be able to find it all in Maple Grove's only general store and that she would not have to travel to another town or to have items ordered in. She was looking forward to making this dress, for it would help her seamstress business grow, as word got around about her talents at sewing clothes, since Mrs. Porter had many friends.

Amanda breathed a sigh of relief, as she saw the green-plaid fabric, that she had in mind, was available. She was able to find buttons and lace that would work perfectly with the fabric. Although she couldn't see ribbon that would match, she thought she might have some in her own, dress-shop supplies. Amanda brushed away some strands of dark brown hair out of her eyes that had escaped her bun due to the Texas wind in the short walk across the street from her dress shop to the general store. As she started to gather what she needed, she felt a presence behind her, and she knew immediately who it was.

She turned around to face the last person she wanted to see that day and the person she was hoping to avoid. Craig Parker was standing in front of her with a new shovel and a bag of nails in his hands.

"Hello, Amanda," Craig greeted her with his big booming voice and teasing grin. Amanda couldn't help but notice his sun-bleached-blond hair that desperately needed a trim and his surprisingly bright, sky-blue eyes. He had removed his cowboy hat which was tucked under his arm.

"Hello, Mr. Parker," Amanda tried to answer quietly, so they wouldn't attract attention from the shopkeeper, Mrs. Estelle Davis. Mrs. Davis, in Amanda's opinion, happened to be the biggest gossip in Maple Grove. She said his last name pointedly, reminding him that she had not given him permission to call her by her first name.

Craig just grinned down at her, looking delighted that he had the opportunity to talk to her. "Have you thought more about my proposal of marriage?" he asked her, his voice sounding a little quieter but still loud just the same.

"The answer is still no," Amanda whispered irritably. "Please don't ask me again."

She walked over to a display of sewing scissors and threads, pretending interest in the variety of choices. She tried to hint to Craig to leave her alone and that she wasn't interested in talking about it, especially in the general store.

"I don't see why you won't even consider it," Craig pretended to pout, as he followed her. "I know for a fact you have no other prospects, you being a widow and all, and childless besides." Craig pushed himself between the display and Amanda.

"My decision as to why doesn't concern you," Amanda loudly whispered again. She tried not to look at him because, for some reason every time she did, her heart would do a little flip. The last thing she wanted was to feel an attraction to a man other than her late husband, David.

"Well, I guess if you want to go through life as an old maid, it's your choice," Craig teased her. "But my offer still stands. I have purchased a great little farm that is located just outside of town, you know, but it's kind of lonely out there, and I could use some help."

"You don't marry someone just to have extra help," Amanda said firmly. "You should marry only if you love that person."

"Ah, love," Craig said, his eyes still twinkling with laughter. "That will come after we get to know each other." Craig reached down and handed Amanda a pair of scissors that she had been pretending to study. "Besides, if you marry me, you won't have to work in that shop of yours anymore. You would have someone else to support you."

Craig's words frustrated Amanda and made her more determined not to marry him. She knew Craig had no idea that she didn't have to work. David had left her a sizable amount of money when he had died, along with the small house that she was living in. After his death, Amanda had decided to turn part of her home into a dress shop and to sew clothes for other women and children. She loved to sew, and it kept her busy. Sewing also made her feel close to David, as he had purchased the Singer sewing machine for her as a gift for their fifth-wedding anniversary.

Amanda had loved David very much and didn't think she could ever love another man. She had resigned herself to the fact that she would live alone for the rest of her life. If only she had been able to have a child with David, then she wouldn't be so lonely. But it wasn't meant to be, and she had long ago accepted her childless state.

Amanda felt angry with Craig because she was afraid he was just looking for another free "ranch hand" to work to death, like what had happened to her mother. Amanda's father had died when she was a young girl. Her mother had remarried soon after, mainly because she couldn't support Amanda on her own and care for the farm that she and her first husband had purchased before Amanda was born.

Her new stepfather was a very stern man and kept her mother and Amanda working and busy all day long and sometimes even late into the night. Despite all their hard work, there was never enough to eat, and the small farm home they lived in was crumbling around them. Her mother died when Amanda was sixteen years old, probably from exhaustion. She went to bed one night after an extremely hard day's work and never woke up.

Amanda left the farm on her own soon after her mother's funeral and was able to find work as a kitchen maid in David's family home. Even though it wasn't the proper thing to do, David and Amanda fell in love and married when she was eighteen years old. She had many fond memories of her marriage to David. He was almost ten years older than she was. He was an attorney, and they had moved to Maple Grove, Texas, soon after they had married. He died from falling off of a horse and hitting his head on a rock when he was on his way home from visiting a client on a ranch near Maple Grove. They had been married for eight years. She had since been alone the last two years and planned on being by herself for the rest of her life.

Chapter 2

AMANDA NOTICED A COMMOTION at the front counter of the general store. She could see a group of ladies crowding around the counter, with Mrs. Estelle Davis behind it talking loudly, waving her arms around as she spoke. Amanda put the scissors that Craig had given her back on the display rack and gathered up her chosen fabric and notions. She walked towards the counter to see what was going on, leaving Craig to follow if he wished.

When she approached the counter, she leaned over to one side and noticed a large poster lying on the scarred counter. It said "Wanted: Homes for Orphan Children." The words confused her.

"What does the poster mean?" she asked a nearby woman who happened to be one of her neighbors, Mrs. Charlotte Moss. Mrs. Moss and her husband ran a bakery that was located next door to her dress shop.

"A group of orphans are coming to Maple Grove on the train in a few days from New York," Mrs. Moss explained as the women around them continued talking. "Evidently these children are from an orphanage called 'The Children's Aid Society.' They all have lost their own parents for some reason or another, and they need new families."

"Orphan trains have been taking children to new families for the last ten years or so," the doctor's wife, Mrs. Pamela Collins, added to their conversation. "The train drops them off to different farming communities and families are given a chance to adopt them. If some of the children aren't placed, they get back on the train and go to the next town."

The reverend's wife, Mrs. Abby Watson, added further to the conversation. "There will be about eighteen children coming here to Maple Grove in a few days. It would be wonderful if all eighteen were placed in our own community."

"May I see the poster?" Amanda asked Mrs. Davis. She handed the poster to Amanda, as she continued to loudly let everyone know that she and her husband planned on doing their duty in taking a child.

Amanda leaned over the poster in her hand and faintly noticed Craig, standing beside her reading along with her.

WANTED: Homes for 18 orphan children!
A group of orphan children from the Children's Aid Society of New York will arrive in Maple Grove, Texas.
These children are intelligent, well disciplined, and in good health. There will be both boys and girls of various ages. A local committee from Maple Grove will help assist in selecting the families in which to place these children. Applications will be accepted on Wednesday, May 24th, at 10:00 a.m. in the Town Hall. The children will arrive on Friday, May 26th, and will be available to meet in the Town Hall at 11:00 a.m. Come see and meet these children and hear the address of Mr. Thomas Carver, the children's placing agent, along with his wife Mrs. Darlene Carver.

AMANDA LOOKED UP, AMAZED that this event was even happening. She handed the poster back to Mrs. Davis and silently listened to the chatter of the other women. She learned that most of them were wanting to take a child.

Eventually the women drifted away from the counter, and Amanda was able to purchase the supplies she needed. As she left the store, Craig placed his purchases down on the counter and ran after her.

"Maybe I will take a boy since you keep refusing my offer," Craig said to Amanda, as he rushed to open the store door for her.

"It would be irresponsible to adopt a child just to work for you!" Amanda said forcefully to him, as they stepped outside in the Texas sunshine.

For the first time, Craig looked angry. "If you think that is the only reason why I would want a boy, you don't know me at all." He turned and walked back into the store to pay for his purchases.

Amanda sighed with relief that Craig was finally leaving her alone and walked the short distance to her shop. Once inside, she put away her purchases and walked over to her sewing machine to continue her work on a light-green dress she was making for a little girl. As she worked on the hem, she thought over the events of the afternoon. She felt so frustrated that Craig kept pursuing her. She had no plans to marry again, and she definitely wouldn't marry unless there was love between them like there had been between David and her.

She started to think about the orphan train and the eighteen children who would soon be visiting the town and quite possibly staying. What if she tried to apply for a child, a little girl? Why not a widow like herself?

I would be a good parent, she thought to herself. *I have a lot of love to give. There might be a little girl who would be happy with just having a new mother. I could provide a suitable home and could even teach her how to sew, so she would have a skill to use when she was older. It would be better for a child to have one parent than no parent at all.*

As Amanda made plans to submit an application for a child, she felt a peace in her heart that this was the right thing to do.

CRAIG HURRIED BACK into the store to purchase the items he needed for his farm. He couldn't believe Amanda would think so little of him that he would want a child just to work the farm. Who did she think he was? She really didn't know him for her to make a judgment like that.

Craig was ready to settle down and start a family. He started having this desire when he first met Amanda at a barn raising a year ago. She was the most beautiful woman he had ever seen, with her dark-brown hair and almost black eyes. Her hair had some red streaks in it that shown in the sun. Her hair was always in place just right, and she always wore beautiful dresses, most likely wearing the clothing she had made herself.

He climbed on his horse and headed north out of Maple Grove. As he rode along, he started to calm down, and he thought more seriously of adopting a boy. Would it even be a good idea? He didn't need a boy to work the farm. He had his friend and his wife helping him. John Sitting Horse had worked with him for a number of years on various cattle ranches around Texas and the surrounding states. When Craig purchased his farmland, he asked John to live on his land and help him. John recently married a woman named Lily. John acted as a foreman rather than a hired hand. Craig provided John and Lily with a small house and food. He also paid them a small salary. Lily helped keep Craig's farmhouse clean and did all the cooking.

He didn't need Amanda to help keep house. He admitted to himself that he was lonely and that he was ready to marry and start a family, but Amanda had rejected his proposal of marriage many times. He had thought he just needed to be patient, that Amanda just needed convincing, and some more time to get over her husband's death. Maybe he should just admit defeat and look to see if there were other available ladies around whom he might want to marry.

But no, he only wanted Amanda. *I'll keep trying to get to know her,* he decided. *I just need to be more patient. I am going to see if there will be a boy from the orphan train who would like to live on a farm. Maybe he won't care if he only has a father as his new family.*

Craig rode his horse onto his farmland and stopped in front of his house. He slid off his horse and tied the reins to a fence. It was almost lunchtime, so he decided to get something to eat before he headed out to help John with some fencing.

Craig stood and looked at his two-story house. It was a large home, too large for one man. The previous owner had had a large family, so there were six bedrooms upstairs. The kitchen was a nice size to cook in. Lily had told him she loved to work in his kitchen because there was so much room to move around from one project to another and so many places to store a variety of food. There was a room off the kitchen that could be used as a parlor if he had a wife who would want to use it as such. There was another smaller room he used as an office and to keep track of his farm finances. He spent most of his time in this room when he was in his home. There was a large built-in bookcase on one end of the room where he was slowly collecting good books to read.

Yes, Craig thought to himself. *I need to start filling this house up, and I might as well start with an orphan boy.*

Chapter 3

THE NEXT DAY, AMANDA woke up early so she could get ready to meet with the Town Committee about adopting a little girl. After her husband had died, she had converted the parlor into a dressing room where her customers could try on dresses, and she could take their measurements. There were two large mirrors and a small area she had blocked off with a movable wall to be used as a small changing area. Opposite of the mirrors were her sewing machine and a long table where she cut fabric.

She kept the kitchen for herself and a small room off the kitchen as her bedroom that her husband had used as a study and office. She had another room located behind the parlor where she stored her fabrics and notions, so her customers had something to immediately choose from. This room used to be the bedroom she had shared with David.

Amanda decided to wear a forest green dress with black trim that was more suited to colder weather, but she chose to wear this dress to meet with the Town Committee because she felt it made her look her best. She brushed out her long brown hair and put it up in her usual bun on the back of her head. She slipped on her sturdy black shoes, and then she was ready to go.

When she opened the door to leave, she saw a woman walking on the pathway that led to her house. It was the mayor's wife, Mrs. Margaret Porter.

"I am so glad I caught you!" Mrs. Porter exclaimed, as she approached. "I do hope you haven't purchased the fabric yet, because I want to make some changes to the dress I ordered a few days ago." Mrs. Porter walked right into the house without being invited, continuing to talk as she did.

"Last night I was talking to my dear friend, Mrs. Mabel Brown, you know who she is, don't you?" Mrs. Porter walked over and sat down on a chair that Amanda had set up for her customers, continuing to talk without waiting for an answer from Amanda.

"She told me that I should include some more lace around the collar, and I shouldn't have as much ribbon. She says that the styles are constantly changing in the East, and this way my new dress will be exactly like they wear back there."

Amanda followed Mrs. Porter into her sewing room, sighing silently to herself. She hoped she could get Mrs. Porter to leave before too long, so that she wouldn't miss being able to talk to the committee. Mrs. Porter did love to talk, and talk she did for the next thirty minutes.

When Mrs. Porter finally left, after making the decision to stay with the original plans for the dress, Amanda sighed to herself in relief. She should still be able to make it. She grabbed a shawl and quickly left her house, before another customer showed up.

She quickly walked to the Town Hall and into the big room where the town meetings were held. In the middle of the room was a large table with five men sitting behind it. There was the mayor, Mr. Richard Porter; the reverend, Mr. Owen Watson; Dr. Brad Collins; and two other men who worked with the mayor and did not contribute to the interview. One of the men listened to the proceedings, and the other was busy writing.

Amanda introduced herself, though most of the men knew who she was. The mayor invited her to sit down on a chair in front of them.

"Tell us why you feel you would be a good candidate as a mother to an orphan child," the reverend requested.

Amanda proceeded to tell the men a brief history of her marriage and then death of her husband and how lonely she has been since. She talked about how she regretted not being able to have children with David and how she thought she had a lot she could contribute to an orphan girl. She would love her, educate her, and even teach her the skills of sewing, so the child would be able to contribute to society and have the means to support herself when she was grown.

After Amanda finished talking, each of the men were given an opportunity to ask her questions. One question posed by the mayor was about finances, and Amanda was able to reassure the men that she could support a child without any outside help.

Then the doctor spoke. "I think we should grant Mrs. Drake her wish to adopt a child." He looked at the other men. "Although she is a woman and single, I think she will do well as a mother, and remember we did give Mr. Craig Parker permission to adopt."

The other men nodded their heads in agreement. Then the mayor spoke directly to Amanda. "You have our permission to adopt a girl who is under five years of age, but you must allow the couples to choose first. If there is a child left, she may be placed with you."

Amanda left the Town Hall five minutes later with a paper in her hands with the committee's agreement that she could adopt a little girl. She stopped outside of the building and opened up the paper to read it. She felt relieved that she had been granted permission, and even though she would need to wait until all the other couples had chosen, she felt very hopeful there would be a child she could adopt.

"It looks like the committee voted in your favor like they did me," Craig stood in front of her holding his own copy of an agreement.

"Yes, I am so excited!" Amanda told him, briefly forgetting her irritation with him and the continued marriage proposals. "They will place a little girl with me as long as she is under five years old and as long as none of the couples have chosen her."

Her dark eyes sparkled with excitement, and Craig thought to himself that he had never seen her as beautiful as she was at that moment.

Amanda then looked at the paper Craig was holding and some of her excitement died. "So you are also going to try to adopt?"

"Yes, I have been approved to get an older boy eight years of age or older."

"Please don't use him like a hired hand," Amanda pleaded to him. and Craig stepped away from her with a frown on his face.

"Since you refuse to marry me, I might as well adopt a child. At least then I will have someone to talk to and share my house with," Craig retorted, tired of her accusing him of not being able to care for a child properly. He put his papers in his pocket and walked away, leaving Amanda staring after him with her mouth open.

Maybe he is as lonely as I am, Amanda thought to herself, and for the first time she felt like, maybe, they did have something in common after all.

Chapter 4

FRIDAY AFTERNOON FINALLY came. Never had time traveled so slowly for Amanda. She did her best to keep herself busy. She finished the child's dress she was working on and started cutting out the fabric for Mrs. Porter's dress. She also found time to make a small dress for her new daughter, hoping that she would be able to really give it to someone and that it would be the right size. At the last minute on Thursday evening, she made a small rag doll with a matching dress for the child.

About ten minutes before two o'clock, Amanda left her dress shop and walked quickly to the Town Hall down the street. She walked into the building and into the room where she was interviewed a few days before. Numerous chairs had been set up in rows and a small stage had been placed in the front of the room with many chairs set up in a row. They were still empty, so Amanda knew that the children hadn't arrived yet.

She looked around and was amazed at the number of people in the room. She recognized many people, but there were several people she didn't know. *Surely not everyone here wants a child,* she hoped. She waved to her good friend, Lydia and her husband, Clinton Byron. They owned a large cattle ranch located south of Maple Grove. Amanda walked over to where they were sitting.

Lydia stood as Amanda approached to give her a hug. "It is so good to see you," Lydia said. "I hope everything is going well."

"Things are fine," Amanda hugged Lydia back and smiled at Clinton in greeting. "Are you considering adopting a child?"

Lydia looked at Clinton as she answered. "Yes, we hope we can find a baby or a young child under two years of age."

"We have a huge house and the ranch. We figure we have enough to offer a child who doesn't have a family," Clinton explained.

"That's great," Amanda said, very happy for her friend. She knew that Lydia had had several miscarriages and had been unable to carry a child to term. Lydia never looked very happy or at peace whenever Amanda saw her, although she always denied her unhappiness. Amanda hoped adopting a baby would help fill some of the emptiness Lydia seemed to display.

Amanda held up her papers. "I was accepted to take a little girl under five years, if there is one left after all the couples have chosen."

Lydia shrieked with joy and hugged Amanda again. "That is great. I hope it works out for you."

"I'm not sure if I will get a child though," Amanda looked around the crowded room. "There are many more people here than I'd expected."

"Oh, I wouldn't worry too much about that," Lydia waved her hand. "I suspect most of these people are just here to watch."

Amanda was shocked at the thought. "How awful! Do they think these children are a bunch of animals? They shouldn't be allowed here if they aren't serious about adopting."

"Well, as much as I agree with you, you have to admit this is a rare occasion. If we weren't planning on taking a baby, I would have been tempted to watch."

Amanda looked around and saw some of the Town Committee walking to the front of the room. "I want to sit closer so I can see the children better." She pointed to the front row of chairs. "I think I will go sit over there."

She said her goodbyes and good lucks to her friends and walked over to the row of chairs that was closest to the stage as possible. Most of the chairs were taken, but then she saw that one was not, and it happened to be right next to Craig Parker.

Amanda hesitated, not wanting to sit next to Craig but wanting to sit as close as possible. He then spotted her and waved his hand for her to come over to him.

"I saved you a seat, since I knew you would want to sit next to me," he explained when she reached his side.

Amanda started to make a sharp retort, but then saw the usual twinkle in his blue eyes and knew he was teasing her again, so she just smiled and sat down.

"Thank you, Mr. Parker."

Craig smiled at the use of his formal name.

The minute she sat down, the hall quieted, as the doors opened, and a tall, thin man and heavy-set woman walked into the room leading a group of children. Amanda noticed that the man was holding a little girl who was big enough to walk. The plump woman was holding the hands of two other young girls. They all walked to the front of the room, and the woman started to direct the children to sit in the chairs on the stage. Amanda watched as three older girls that looked to be the same age sat next to each other. They were each holding a baby or toddler. The man sat the little girl he was holding on a chair, and an older boy immediately sat next to her, grabbing her hand with his own.

They must be brother and sister, Amanda thought. *I hope they won't be separated.* She then noticed that the little girl's left leg was twisted.

After all the children had sat down, Amanda quickly counted that there were only four girls that looked to be under the age of five, counting the little girl with the twisted leg. There were two babies, but she had decided she wanted a child older than two-years old. Five girls to choose from didn't seem very many, and Amanda's heart sunk, knowing she probably would not be able to take a child home with her.

"Don't give up hope yet," Craig whispered to her, letting her know he knew what her thoughts were. She smiled her appreciation. When she looked at him, she couldn't help but notice his broad shoulders that filled out under his blue shirt. He had gotten his hair cut, and there was a lock of hair sticking straight up that made Amanda want to reach up and smooth it into place. Realizing her thoughts, her heart fluttered again. Amanda quickly looked away, silently telling herself to not get caught up in his good looks and charm.

The mayor stood and introduced the man and woman as Mr. and Mrs. Thomas Carver. He explained that this couple had been with the children on the train ever since they had left New York ten days ago. The mayor then announced that Mr. Carver had some instructions to give, allowed the man to take his place, and sat down in the front row next to his wife.

Mr. Carver stood and began to speak. "I welcome you all, and I am thrilled with the interest and turnout we have this afternoon. This is truly a wondrous event for the children and for the town of Maple Grove. I want to thank the Town Committee for their part in helping these, beautiful children find new homes.

"I know that everyone is anxious to begin, so those that have been approved can be matched with a child, but I must go over some ground rules and procedures. There are two key points.

"These girls and boys are hoping to find a new home. We have eighteen children available between the ages of six months and fourteen years of age. We are hopeful that all eighteen will be placed right here in Maple Grove, but if that doesn't happen, we will continue onto the next town until they are all placed.

"We are allowing the children eight and older to make the decision whether they want to go with a family. If they feel uncomfortable in any way, we will not force them to go. The final decision is theirs. There will be a one-year waiting period between child placement and legal adoption. We will be sending out a representative a few times in the next year to check on the children. If at any time we feel dissatisfied with the child's care, we will remove the child from the home. Please be aware that even though this is rare, it has happened."

Mr. Carver paused in his speaking to pull a handkerchief from his pocket to wipe perspiration from his neck and brow.

"In order to avoid mass confusion, we will call each name who has a letter of recommendation in random order. Once a choice has been made, please move over to where my wife is sitting, and she will help you complete the paperwork." He pointed to a table that had been set up to one side of the room with Mrs. Carver sitting behind it.

Mr. Carver then called the first name which happened to be the reverend and his wife. With them was their teenage son. Amanda watched as their son walked right up to a young girl who looked to be about six years old. He squatted in front of her and started to talk to her.

Chapter 5

AMANDA SAT QUIETLY in her chair, watching, as one by one each child was paired up with a family. She noticed that no one tried talking to the little girl with the twisted leg.

At one point, the blacksmith and his wife tried to talk to the boy sitting next to the little girl with the twisted leg, and Amanda heard the boy yell, "I don't want to go with anyone! I don't want a new family!"

Mr. Carver walked over to try to calm the boy, but it was obvious he would not agree, so the blacksmith and his wife walked over to another boy.

Craig leaned over to Amanda and whispered, "I am going to adopt that boy."

Amanda looked at him in amazement. "He seems so angry. Why would you want to have a boy that is displaying behavioral problems?"

"He just needs someone who will care about him. He'll settle down. I believe I can help that boy." While Craig was talking, he kept his eyes on the events on the stage, but then he turned to look directly at Amanda. For the first time, she saw that he felt very deeply about the proceedings, and they were very important to him.

"I'm not the heartless man you seem to think I am. A little hard work has never hurt anyone, but I don't plan on working the boy too hard. He needs acceptance and a place to belong. He will have that with me."

Amanda felt confusion as she turned her head back towards the stage and pondered Craig's words. *Maybe*, she thought, *he really could provide a good home for an orphan boy. Maybe I have been too harsh, too critical of him as a man, because of the many times he has proposed to me. It all seemed like a big joke to him. Maybe he really does want to marry me.*

Soon there were only three children left. Of course, the boy who yelled at the blacksmith was still there, still clutching the hand of the little girl beside him. There was also another boy sitting on a chair a few seats down the row, looking sad, as he stared at the floor.

Mr. Carver called her name and Craig's. They both jumped up and walked onto the stage.

"It seems there is a little girl left," Mr. Carver said to Amanda. "I need to warn you though, she can barely walk without pain. Her leg was injured in a wagon accident that took her parents' lives when she was two-years old. It hasn't healed properly." Mr. Carver pointed to the boy sitting next to the little girl. "That boy is her big brother."

"What are their names?" Amanda asked.

"Jeremy and Grace."

"Would you like to come live with me on my farm?" Craig walked up and asked the boy.

"I keep telling everyone, I don't want a new family!" The boy hollered again with a frown on his face.

Mr. Carver put his hand on the boy's shoulder and started to reprimand him, but Craig held his hand out to silence the agent.

"Tell us why. You have to have a reason for not wanting a new family."

The boy looked at Craig suspiciously, as if he didn't believe Craig cared about his reasons. Craig stood patiently waiting for his answer.

"I don't want to be separated from Grace. She and I are all we have left of our family." He finally responded with defiance in his voice.

Mr. Carver leaned close to Craig. "We have explained to him that being able to stay together will likely not happen. The best he can hope for is if they both go to families who live close by, and they can visit."

"How old is Grace?" Amanda asked the agent.

"She is four years old," he replied.

"Tell us why it is so important you stay together," Craig requested of Jeremy. "Why is it so important that you might be giving up a chance for a new family for yourself and for your little sister who could be cared for?"

"After Grace was born, Ma was always sickly. Pa told me my sister was my responsibility and that I was to take care of her if anything happened to my ma or him." The boy looked bravely at Craig, blinking back tears from his eyes. "I promised him I would. I can't break my promise to my pa." The boy's eyes pleaded with Craig to understand.

Amanda turned to Mr. Carver. "If I wanted to, would I be able to adopt Grace?" she asked, needing to make sure.

Mr. Carver nodded. "You can adopt her, but remember that Grace will need a lot of care, and there could be more expenses you will need to pay for because of her leg."

"That won't be a problem. I have the means to do so," Amanda answered.

She missed seeing a surprised look from Craig, when he heard her admit that money would not be a problem. She stood and quietly looked at the little girl. She had long, blond, curly hair that desperately needed a brush. The dress was a dull brown, and it was too large for her. But Grace glanced up at her with such a sweet, shy smile, which made Amanda immediately fall in love with her.

Craig and Mr. Carver were still trying to convince Jeremy to change his mind. While Amanda was thinking, she noticed another couple who already had a passel of children walk off the stage with the last boy who had been sitting by himself.

"We always have room for one more," the woman boomed out with her arm around his shoulders. "You'll have more brothers and sisters than you will know what to do with, and you can have a place with us for as long as you want it."

Amanda then knew what she had to do. "Mr. Parker, may I talk to you for a minute?"

Craig looked confused, but nodded. "If you would excuse us."

Mr. Carver nodded his head, as Amanda and Craig returned to the seats they had been sitting in.

"It looks like I will be able to adopt Grace," Amanda said to Craig as soon as they were seated. "And you want to adopt Jeremy."

Craig nodded. "I will if I can get Jeremy to agree. We would need to make sure they visit each other often."

Amanda looked down at her lap, hoping she was making the right decision. "Do you still want to marry me?"

Craig looked at her in disbelief, as if he wasn't sure he had heard her correctly, and then he smiled with delight. "Yes, I still want to marry you."

"Then I accept your proposal. We can both adopt Jeremy and Grace, and then they can stay together. Jeremy can keep his promise he made to his father."

"That is a great idea," Craig said. "When do you want to marry?"

"It probably should happen soon, don't you think? So they can stay together."

"How about today?"

Amanda took a huge breath and then nodded. Everything was happening so fast. But she needed to marry him, so the children could stay together. She felt a peace in her heart that this decision was right for all four of them.

"Would you be willing to live on my farm?" Craig asked.

"Of course, Mr. Parker. My shop is too small for the four of us." Amanda replied. "I would like to keep my sewing business though."

Craig looked like he was going to argue but then backed down. "That's fine, although I think it's time you call me Craig, don't you?"

Amanda nodded her head in agreement and smiled at him. He took her hand and squeezed it, and Amanda felt another stirring in her heart for this man who had relentlessly pursued her for the past year. A caring started to take root in her heart, and she could not stop it.

"Let's go let everyone know our decision," Craig kept Amanda's hand in his, as he led her to the children and Mr. Carver.

"Mrs. Drake and I have been able to come up with a way we can all be happy," Craig looked at both children as he spoke. "I have been asking her to marry me for quite some time now, and she finally accepted. We will be married today, and then we can adopt you both. This way you can keep your promise to your father, Jeremy, and you can both stay together."

"Do you mean it?" Jeremy asked in disbelief. "You would marry, so we can stay together?"

"Yes," Amanda answered. "We would like all of us to be a family."

"Is that an acceptable plan, young man?" Mr. Carver asked, with a twinkle in his eyes, happy that things were working out for everyone.

"Yes, sir."

"Then let's get the paperwork done, so your new mom and dad can get married."

Craig picked up Grace, and they all moved over to the table where Mrs. Carver was sitting. They quickly filled out the necessary paperwork. As soon as the last paper was signed, Craig motioned to the doors.

"Let's go get married!" he said with excitement, and they started down the street towards the reverend's home to make the vows to become a family.

Chapter 6

AMANDA AND CRAIG WALKED down the street towards the church and parsonage. Craig held Grace while Jeremy walked beside them. Amanda noticed that Jeremy's eyes looked happier, like a huge load had been lifted from his shoulders.

When they got to the parsonage and knocked on the door, the reverend's wife, Mrs. Abby Watson, answered. She looked happy to see them, but she had a question in her eyes, as she let them in.

Mrs. Watson led them into a parlor and told them to sit down on a gray-colored sofa. Craig kept Grace on his lap, and Jeremy sat between them. Amanda noticed Jeremy looking around the room in awe, as if he couldn't believe how nice the furniture was. A gray sofa was perched at the edge of a large, colorful area rug. There was another, smaller sofa on the opposite side of the room with a wooden table in front of it. The fireplace had a mantle made out of maple wood above it. On the mantle was a large clock and a few knick-knacks. Above the mantle was a large, oval mirror with a gilded frame. The walls had been papered with a rose-covered design. It really was a beautiful room.

"We are looking for Reverend Watson," Craig explained. "We have decided to get married, and we would like it to be done today." While he was talking, the reverend came into the room.

"What's this I hear about getting married?" Reverend Watson asked with a smile.

"Amanda and I have adopted these two children, and we would like to marry, so we can be a family."

The reverend looked carefully at Craig and then at Amanda. He finally nodded, as if he liked what he saw, and he had received the answer he was looking for.

"Although I generally give counsel to have an engagement of at least a few months, and I like to meet with each couple before marriage, I do approve of this one. I will be happy to perform the marriage. I understand why it needs to be rushed," the reverend said, as he shook hands with Craig and then Jeremy. "Today is your lucky day," he said to the boy.

Jeremy nodded his head in agreement. "My new dad and mom have agreed to marry so Grace and I can stay together."

"Well, there are other reasons I want to marry Amanda," Craig looked at her with his usual teasing grin. "I didn't think she'd ever agree to marry me. I should have thought to throw a few children into the proposals. We would have been married long ago."

Amanda looked down in embarrassment. Did he have to announce how many times he had asked her, and she had turned him down? She felt a touch on her sleeve.

"Congratulations," Mrs. Watson said softly to her. "I think you will be happy. Mr. Parker is a fine man."

Amanda smiled her appreciation and started to say something when they were interrupted by the reverend and Abby's teenage son, Benjamin.

"Ma, I think Mary is done with her meal and is tired. Can I show her the room we prepared for her?"

"Yes, I will go with you. I am sure this has been a tiring day for her." Mrs. Watson looked at her husband and then at Amanda and Craig. "Please excuse me."

After Mrs. Watson left, Amanda turned to the reverend. "I noticed that you and Mrs. Watson also adopted an orphan."

"Yes, we did," the reverend responded. "We have always wanted another child, but the good Lord has only blessed us with Benjamin. He has been asking for a little sister ever since he was small. We decided we would allow him to choose one of the orphans for his sister, and he chose Mary."

"I'm sure Mary will be happy living here with you and your family," Amanda said. "I am sure all the orphans were able to fine good homes right here in Maple Grove and in the surrounding area."

"That's good to hear," the reverend said. "We will have to help each other and do what we can to make this town the best place for them to live in."

"So will you marry us now?" Craig asked, getting the conversation back to the reason they had come in the first place.

"Yes, I will," the reverend agreed. "We need witnesses. Will you mind if we just perform it here in our parlor instead of the church? That way Abby and Benjamin can be the witnesses, and they can stay nearby if Mary needs them."

Both Amanda and Craig agreed to the plan. The reverend left the room and soon returned with his wife and son. He asked Amanda and Craig to stand near the fireplace. Grace stood next to Amanda and Jeremy stood next to Craig. The reverend picked up the Bible and started the wedding ceremony.

While Reverend Watson talked, Amanda tried to concentrate on the words but could not. She found herself comparing the difference between her first wedding and this one to Craig. She and David had eloped because his family was against the wedding. They had been married in the local courthouse, but Amanda hadn't cared. She loved David so much, she was just happy to be marrying him. They had had a good life together and had been very happy. Would she be able to have a good marriage with Craig?

Amanda looked into Craig's eyes. He was looking down at her, and she saw something in his eyes that she never thought she would see again. She could tell he deeply cared about her. This marriage, even though it was happening because of the children, meant something to him. For the first time, Amanda felt regret for putting him off and rejecting his proposals for so long. She knew that he was a good man, and he would treat her and the children well.

At that moment, as she repeated her marriage vows to Craig in front of the reverend, his wife and son, and her new children, she vowed that she would do everything she could to be a good wife to Craig and a good mother to Jeremy and Grace. Hopefully, someday she would feel love for him.

When the time came to exchange rings, Amanda and Craig looked at each other. Neither of them had thought of rings. Amanda looked down at her left hand and saw that she still wore the ring that David had given her. She immediately struggled to take it off in embarrassment. Craig stopped her.

"It's okay," he whispered. He then turned to the reverend. "We will use this one for now."

The reverend nodded and continued the ceremony. Then Amanda heard the words, "You may now kiss the bride."

Amanda jerked her head and looked up at Craig. Was he really going to kiss her? As he bent his head toward hers, she suddenly realized she wanted to experience his first kiss, even in front of so many witnesses.

Craig's lips touched hers softly. Then suddenly his arms went around her, and he deepened the kiss. It only lasted a second, but in that moment Amanda felt feelings toward Craig that she had never felt before. When he stepped away, she had to force herself to not lift her hand to touch her lips in wonder. Could a simple kiss, a wedding kiss really mean so much? Why did her heart flutter at the thought of kissing him again?

Craig was shaking the preacher's hand and thanking Mrs. Watson and Benjamin for being part of the wedding. He had taken Amanda's hand after the kiss, and he kept holding it until they were ready to leave the parsonage.

Abby had offered to serve refreshments, but both Amanda and Craig declined.

"We have so much we need to do before we can head out to the farm," Craig explained, while Amanda nodded her head in agreement.

"You need to spend time with your new daughter," Amanda said, "and we have some shopping to do for our new son and daughter." She turned to look at her children as she spoke.

Soon they were out the door and on their way to the general store; a new marriage, a new family, a new life.

Chapter 7

"THAT DIDN'T TAKE VERY long," Jeremy said with some relief in his voice, and Craig chuckled.

"Are you my new mommy?" Grace asked Amanda from her place in Craig's arms, and Amanda nodded.

"Is that okay, sweetie?"

Grace nodded, but looked down at her brother for confirmation.

"Sure, Grace, these people are our new ma and pa. We won't have to go back and live in that orphanage again."

Grace looked relieved at his words and laid her head on Craig's shoulder.

"We really should pick up some supplies for these two and then go to my shop so I can pack a few things to take to your farm," Amanda suggested.

"Our farm," Craig corrected her, and she smiled. "Grace looks tired. Should we go to your house first, so she can rest for a bit?"

"That sounds like a good idea," Amanda agreed. They quickly walked to her shop, and she led them all inside.

Jeremy immediately started looking around, making himself at home. Amanda led Craig to her small bedroom behind the kitchen and indicated he could lay Grace down on the bed.

"Why don't you go to sleep for a little while?" Amanda suggested to Grace, who nodded her head in agreement and closed her eyes.

Soon she was sound asleep. Amanda lightly brushed some of her blond, curly hair from her face, marveling that she now had her own daughter and son. She was amazed how quickly things could change. She stood up quickly and turned around, bumping into Craig who had been standing behind her.

"Oh, I thought you had left to go see to Jeremy," Amanda stuttered breathlessly, feeling flustered that they were standing so close together. Her room was so tiny. There was barely room for her bed and a small chest for her clothes.

Craig started to answer and then stopped. His hand reached up and brushed some strands of hair from her face, much like she had just done to Grace.

"The kiss I gave you at the reverend's house didn't seem quite right. I'd like to try again." Time seemed to stop, as Amanda watched his eyes move to look at her lips, then back to her eyes. He slowly bent his head, and she tilted her face in anticipation.

"Man, you sure have a lot of fabric here," Amanda heard Jeremy call out. "Is this a store?"

They both jerked their heads away from each other, and Amanda felt a distinct disappointment. For a moment, she wanted to experience his kiss again. She shook her head slightly in confusion. She shouldn't want him to kiss her. Even though they were married, they hardly knew each other.

Craig looked disappointed too, but then he grinned and whispered, "Later." He turned and left the room to find Jeremy.

Amanda sat down on the edge of the small bed and covered her face with her hands. She could faintly hear Craig explain to Jeremy how his new mom had a sewing shop and sewed dresses for some of the women who lived in town. She felt very confused. *I shouldn't be having these feelings for Craig*, she thought. *I was blessed to have love in my first marriage. I am not sure I can feel love for someone else again.* When they were standing so close together, with Craig leaning close ready to kiss her again, she felt his closeness like a touch to her heart.

She did not feel ready to join Craig and Jeremy just yet, so she released her hair from her bun. She picked up her hairbrush and quickly brushed through the tangles and redid her hair. She quickly made sure Grace was still sleeping and left her bedroom.

When Amanda entered her sewing room, Jeremy ran up to her. "Could you make Grace a new dress? She hasn't had a new one in a long time. The dress she has on isn't even hers. Someone gave it to her, and it's very old and too big."

Amanda smiled at her new son and marveled on how much he cared and showed love for his sister. She walked over to her sewing table and picked up the dress she had finished the night before.

"I actually made this dress yesterday, hoping I would be able to give it to my new daughter today."

She showed the dress to Jeremy. It was made from a light-pink fabric with small, red flowers all over it. She had added a ruffle around the hem and sleeves and ribbon at the neck. It had many little buttons that buttoned up the back.

"That's mighty fine work," Craig complimented her.

Amanda smiled her thanks.

She picked up the rag doll with the matching dress to show them. "I made this, too. I think every little girl should have her own doll."

Jeremy nodded his agreement. "Ma had made her one when she was a baby, but I don't know what happened to it. Thank you, ma'am." He looked down, his facing showing some concern.

"Is something bothering you?" Craig asked him.

"I just want to ask that, if this doesn't work out and you might decide you don't want me, will you promise to take care of Grace and always be her ma?" Jeremy looked apprehensive as he talked. "I don't think she remembers our ma, and she should have one."

Amanda sat down on her chair she used to do most of her sewing. "Of course, Jeremy, but..."

Craig interrupted her. "You aren't going to be sent back. We are a family now, and you are an important part of it."

Amanda nodded her head in agreement to Craig's words.

"Maybe," Jeremy didn't look convinced. "But I sometimes can cause trouble, and a lot of people don't seem to like me."

"We can work on that, Jeremy, but I agree with your new dad." Amanda wanted to reach out and hug the boy, but she did not think he would accept it. "We are a family now, and we will stay together."

Jeremy looked a little more relieved at her words, but she knew that they would need to show him they meant their words over time.

"Why don't you come into the kitchen with me," Amanda asked him, "and we can have something to eat. It's almost dinner time, and I bet you are hungry."

Jeremy voiced his agreement and followed her into the kitchen.

With Craig helping, she quickly made a stack of meat sandwiches and sliced up some apples and carrots. Grace woke up a few minutes into their meal, so Amanda gave her some food to eat, too.

While her new family finished their meal, Amanda quickly gathered up necessary supplies and clothes to last her a few days and put them into a carpetbag. She was soon ready. She allowed Jeremy to give Grace the new dress and doll. Amanda was relieved when Grace squealed with joy and hugged the doll to her chest.

"Thank you," Grace whispered shyly to Amanda when her brother prompted her. Then she asked more boldly, "Can I wear the new dress now?"

Amanda consented and took Grace back to the bedroom to help her change. As she slid the old dress off Grace's body, she could see the scars and damage to her leg. She wished there was a way they could help her be able to walk normally. Throughout the afternoon, Amanda had been able to see that Grace could walk, but it was difficult. She seemed to tire easily and preferred to be carried.

The dress fit Grace almost perfectly. It was a little big, but Amanda knew Grace would grow into it. Amanda sighed with relief. She knew she had taken a chance making a dress for a child when she did not know the size and measurements.

Chapter 8

SOON THEY WERE ON THEIR way to the general store which was just down the street.

"Why don't you go in with Jeremy and Grace and see if you can find what they need," Craig suggested. "I have my wagon parked in front the Town Hall. I will go get it and park it in front of the store. That way after we are done here, we can head to the farm."

Amanda nodded her agreement and took both children into the store. She looked around, trying to see who was in the store to help them and saw Mrs. Davis. She noticed a young girl beside her who was listening to Mrs. Davis, as she gave her instructions on how to stock a shelf.

Amanda walked up to the shop owner and smiled at the girl. "Hello, Mrs. Davis. We are here to get a few supplies for Jeremy and Grace."

Mrs. Davis greeted Amanda and replied, "I heard there was a quick wedding this afternoon. Didn't know if I should have believed it though, seeing you have been rejecting poor Mr. Parker for so long. I see you finally came to your senses."

Amanda sighed inwardly and decided not to respond to her broad hint for information. "I see you took one of the children."

"Yes, this is Anna." Mrs. Davis nodded towards the young girl. "It seemed the right thing to do, take in one of the orphans. Besides, it gets kind of quiet around our house, now that our three children are grown and gone, and not one of them staying in Maple Grove."

"Children do seem to do that, grow up and leave to live their own lives," Amanda answered, knowing that was what she did after her mother died. She looked at Anna. "It is nice to meet you. Are you going to work in the store a lot?"

Anna started to answer, but Mrs. Davis jumped in. "She will, yes, when she isn't in school and such."

Amanda kept looking at Anna to see if she felt slighted at being put to work so quickly after being taken in.

"I don't mind, ma'am," the girl answered her unspoken question. "I've never seen so many things in one place before." She looked around in awe.

Amanda turned to her own children. "This is Jeremy and Grace." She introduced them. "Children, this is Mrs. Davis who owns the store with her husband. Did you know Anna at the orphanage before you came here?"

Jeremy shook his head, but Grace nodded.

"I helped with Grace sometimes at the orphanage," Anna explained.

"You mean you weren't with Grace at the orphanage?" Amanda asked Jeremy.

"No," he shook his head. "Most of the time they kept the boys separate from the girls."

"How awful!" Amanda exclaimed. "They should have let your sister stay with you." No wonder Jeremy was so insistent on keeping Grace with him.

Jeremy shrugged. "It was just the way it was."

Amanda decided to change the subject. "I would like to purchase a few things for the children and some fabric. I can sew most of their clothes, but they still need some clothes right away."

Soon a small pile of clothing and other supplies were on top of the counter ready for purchase. Craig walked in and looked at the growing pile. Amanda was a little worried that he would say it was too much, but she planned to pay for part of it.

"Looks like you guys are having fun," Craig said, smiling at Grace, as she showed him her new shoes. Amanda sighed in relief at his words.

"We're just about finished." Amanda placed the last bolt of fabric on the counter.

"Did you each pick out something fun?" Craig asked the children.

Jeremy looked confused. "Fun? What do you mean?"

"You can pick out something you want that has nothing to do with clothes." Craig looked at Amanda, as if hoping she wouldn't disagree with his orders.

"What a great idea," Amanda said, smiling at Craig. "I should have thought of that myself."

"But you're already buying us a lot of stuff. We don't need anything else." Jeremy protested. He had never owned so much before.

"Jeremy, come here," Craig motioned to him. The boy stood before him, as Craig put his hands on his shoulders. "This won't happen every time we come to the store. But for today, because it is such as special day for all of us, you can choose something just for yourself."

Jeremy's eyes lit up, as if he finally realized his new dad was serious. "Come on Grace, let's see what we can find." He took her hand and led her away, keeping his steps to match her slower ones.

Amanda smiled at Craig and then turned to Mrs. Davis. "I think we have everything we need for now. How much do we owe you?"

Mrs. Davis started writing everything down to figure out the cost. Craig pulled out a wad of bills, and Amanda placed her hand on his arm.

"I am planning on paying for some of this," she whispered. "I know it might have been more than what you were planning to spend."

Craig scowled at her. "I will be paying for everything. I realize they need everything you picked out. I wouldn't have had a clue what to get them. It's why I asked you to do it."

"But I do have some money, and I can help," Amanda argued. "Don't you think we should be paying for their care together?"

"No, I don't," Craig said firmly. "You are my wife, and they are my children. It is my responsibility. I will pay for this."

Amanda stood there trying to decide if she should continue to argue or let it go and talk to him about money in a more private setting. After all, he wasn't aware of how much money she had.

Craig gave Estelle some bills and then said to Amanda, "In fact, I want you to pick out a ring, a wedding ring."

Amanda looked at him in astonishment. A ring? But she already wore one. Then she realized she still wore her late husband's ring and knew the time had come to remove it. She nodded her agreement, took off the ring she wore, and slid it into her dress pocket.

"Amazing," Craig joked to Mrs. Davis who was watching the exchange with delight. "She didn't even argue with me. That's a first." He took her arm and led her to the display of rings nearby. "Pick out the one you want."

Amanda found a simple gold ring that looked the least expensive and pointed to it. "I like that one."

Craig immediately dismissed it, knowing she chose it because of the price. "Never mind. I will pick out the ring."

He leaned over her and picked out a beautiful gold ring with a small diamond in the center with what looked like a leaf wrapped around it, also in gold. He slid the ring onto her finger. It fit perfectly.

"Do you like it?" he asked, all teasing gone from his voice.

"Yes, I do," Amanda said and looked up into his eyes. "Thank you." Her throat felt clogged, as if it were hard to breathe.

She felt a tug on her dress and looked down to see Grace staring up at her with Jeremy standing nearby.

"Have you found what you wanted?" she asked them, hoping that her voice sounded steadier than she felt.

Grace was holding a storybook, and Jeremy had a harmonica in his hand. They showed their prizes to Amanda and Craig.

"Those are great choices," Craig said approvingly. "Do you know how to play the harmonica?" he asked Jeremy.

The boy shook his head. "I can learn though."

"I'm sure you can," Craig answered. "I actually know how to play, and I can teach you, if you want me to."

He turned to Grace. "I'm sure your new mom will read to you tonight out of your storybook."

Grace nodded her head in agreement, still feeling too shy to talk.

Within a few minutes, all their purchases had been loaded onto the wagon, the children sitting among them, and they were heading towards their new home.

Chapter 9

IT DID NOT TAKE LONG to get to Craig's farm, as it was located just outside the town. It would only take a little while to ride into town to take care of her shop.

As they drove closer, Amanda started to get more apprehensive. She remembered what it was like living on the farm as a child. She had very few good memories living on that farm. She was always grateful that she had been able to find a job so quickly after leaving when her mother died.

She remembered when she first saw David. He had come home from college, having just finished his schooling to become an attorney. It seemed trite to say it was love at first sight, but that's what happened, for both of them. They tried to keep their relationship a secret, mainly because Amanda did not think his family would accept her, since she was just kitchen help and had grown up on a farm. Finally, she agreed to marry him when she was eighteen. She could not live without David any longer, and David had finally convinced Amanda that he did not care what his family thought. He loved her, and he was going to marry her, with or without their blessing.

What Amanda feared did happen. His parents did not approve, and they threatened to disown him, if he married her. Instead of joining his father's lawyer firm, like his parents had wished, David had taken Amanda to Maple Grove and set up his own office for the town and surrounding community.

A few years later, his family decided to accept David's decision to marry Amanda, and they had a pretty good relationship with his family until David died. Amanda had had little contact with his family since.

The wagon came to a stop, and Amanda was surprised to find that they had arrived. She felt a little guilty thinking about her past. She promised herself that she was embarking on a new life, and she would accept all the changes that came with it, good and bad.

She looked around and then saw her new home. She sighed in relief. It was better than anything she had imagined. It was a large two-story farmhouse. It had been painted white with blue shutters. There was a porch that ran the length of the front of the house with a few chairs sitting on it. Two large cottonwood trees on either side of the house offered shade in the heat of the day. It had many windows, and the house looked like it was well cared for. Behind the house, there was a large barn with a few horses standing nearby, and a man was caring for them.

Craig looked at Amanda. "Does it meet with your approval?" he asked, his voice teasing her again.

All Amanda could do was nod. She could immediately see that she would not be living the hard life her mother had, and neither would the children.

"I didn't expect your house to be so large," Amanda finally said, knowing that Craig was waiting for her to say something.

"The previous owners had themselves a passel of kids, so there is plenty of room. They decided to move to Oregon and take advantage of the free land, so I got a good deal on it. They left most of the furniture and animals." Craig jumped down to the ground and then reached up to lift her down. "There are six bedrooms upstairs. The downstairs has a parlor, a room I use for my study, and a large kitchen. Lily sure enjoys working in the kitchen."

"Who is Lily?" Amanda asked, as she scooped Grace up and followed Craig and Jeremy into the house.

"Lily is my housekeeper. She cooks for me and helps keep the house clean. Her husband, John, helps me on the farm, and is basically my foreman, though I don't call him that." He gestured with his arm to a small home some distance away. "They live in that house over there, but they both help me around the farm."

Amanda closed her eyes and sighed with relief. She was starting to see that marriage to Craig was going to be very different than she had imagined. She followed Craig, as he showed Jeremy and Grace the house. When they were upstairs, he allowed the children to choose their own room from the five empty rooms available. Both children were thrilled with the idea of having their own room, and not needing to share, although Jeremy was probably happier about the idea than Grace.

Each room had a bed and a small table next to it. Amanda noticed that neither room had curtains to cover the windows and knew that she would need to sew some. There was a chest at the end of each bed in which to hold clothes.

While the children were exploring their new rooms, Amanda walked into a room right across the hall from the room Craig was using.

"I can take this room," she announced to Craig.

He looked at her and frowned. "What do you mean, you'll take this room?" he questioned. "You'll sleep with me in my room."

"Craig, I know we are married now, but we hardly know each other." Amanda tried to speak her words softly, so the children didn't hear her. "Don't you think we need some time to get to know each other before, you know..."

"No, I don't," Craig said firmly. "But you seem to need some time. I don't think we should start this marriage off in separate rooms. How about if we share my room and my bed, but I agree to not touch you until you are ready?"

Amanda thought about his idea for a minute and then nodded her head. "Okay, as long as you can keep your promise. We probably should share a room for the children's sake, so they don't get confused, since we are married and all."

Craig wisely kept himself from smiling at her comment about the children. "I promise."

THE REST OF THE EVENING was spent putting their new purchases away and getting to know their new home. Jeremy started to act like a regular boy, as he ran through the house, outdoors around the house, to the barn, and back again. He was thoroughly enjoying himself. He was thrilled to see a black and white dog and spent some time playing with him. Craig explained to Jeremy that the dog's name was Shep, and he helped with herding the cattle when needed, but he was mainly a pet.

Grace stayed close to Amanda, as she put their purchases away, but she seemed more relaxed, as she watched Jeremy run in and out of the house. She started to talk a little bit to her new mom.

That night, after the children were settled down and finally in bed, Amanda and Craig were lying side by side in his bed. Both were silent for quite awhile. Amanda then turned to Craig.

"Thank you for marrying me to keep the children together," she whispered in the darkness.

"I married you for other reasons besides the kids," Craig whispered back. "Remember, I've wanted to marry you for a long time."

"Why did you want to marry me so badly?" Amanda questioned. "I would think you would have given up after a while."

"When I first saw you, I knew you were the woman God had chosen for me," Craig explained.

"When did you first see me? I don't remember it."

"It was at the barn raising the town had for the Powells when their barn burned down. Remember that?"

Amanda did remember it. The event was almost a year ago. She hadn't wanted to go and had only gone because Lydia had made her promise to come. She spent most of her time helping prepare food for the men who were building the barn. There was a dance that evening in the new barn, but Amanda remembered refusing to dance, even though Lydia had encouraged her. She didn't remember seeing Craig at the dance. Her first memory of him was running into him just outside the bakery next door as she was heading out of her house to run an errand about a month after the barn raising.

She remembered that day well. She had been in a hurry to go to the general store because she had run out of a specific color of thread and needed to get more to finish a dress that was supposed to be completed the next day. She was walking quickly and was not watching where she was going. She ran smack right into Craig's chest.

He had caught her, as she stumbled and grinned at her, as if he was delighted she had run into him. After a brief introduction, he immediately had proposed marriage.

"I've had my eye on you, ma'am," Craig had declared, "and I've decided you will make a fine wife."

Amanda had been appalled at his audacity in asking her to marry him so quickly after meeting and had practically run to the general store to get away from him.

"I thought you were so beautiful in that light-blue dress you were wearing. Even though I worked hard on putting up that barn, I was also watching you. I got a black thumb from it, too." Craig chuckled. "You had come to offer water to us men, and I couldn't keep my eyes off you. I swung my hammer to hit a nail and hit my thumb instead."

"So, you wanted to marry me, because you think I am pretty."

"I wanted to marry you because you are beautiful. But I also saw how you worked so hard on helping with the meal, cooking over that fire even when it was so hot that day. I saw you comfort a crying child, holding that child as he fell asleep in your lap. I saw that you made an effort to talk to each woman there. You seemed to know just what to say to make people feel comfortable and welcome, especially the new family that had just moved into the area, the blacksmith family. I decided that day that you were the one I was going to marry."

Amanda was silent for a while and then reached out and found Craig's hand. She whispered to her new husband, "I think I have changed my mind."

"About what?"

"I've decided I don't need some time."

Craig slowly turned to her and pulled her close to him. Amanda started to say something else, but she stopped, as he kissed her, letting her know through his kiss how much he cared for her. As he kissed her, she felt as if the ice around her heart cracked apart, leaving behind a new heart that was starting to heal.

Chapter 10

THE NEXT MORNING, AMANDA woke up and saw that Craig was not in bed with her. He must have already started the day. She got up and quickly dressed. Amanda decided to make her new family breakfast, but when she entered the kitchen, she saw a strange woman standing over the stove frying bacon. She obviously had Native-American heritage. She had jet-black hair that was brushed smooth and braided down her back. She had on a colorful dress with bright blues, reds, and yellows in a fun design.

"You must be Lily," Amanda greeted the woman with a smile.

"Yes, I Lily," the woman spoke in broken English. "Welcome to Craig's house, Craig's new wife, Mrs. Parker. I cook breakfast for you."

Amanda started to tell her she could do it, but then stopped herself. She didn't want to take a job away from someone. "Can I help?" she asked instead.

"No help. I do." Lily continued with her work. Amanda saw that a pot of coffee had been started, and she helped herself to a cup.

"How long have you been working for Craig?" Amanda asked after the silence became too long.

"Not long, two year." Lily held up two fingers. She looked over Amanda's shoulder, so Amanda turned and saw Jeremy standing in the doorway.

"Come sit down, Jeremy," Amanda invited her new son. "This is....what is your last name?" she questioned Lily.

"Husband's name is John Sitting Horse."

"This is Mrs. Sitting Horse," Amanda introduced her to Jeremy.

The young Indian woman shook her head. "Children call me Lily." She smiled at the boy. "Welcome. Breakfast done soon."

Jeremy sat down at the kitchen table. "Is Grace still asleep?" Amanda asked.

Jeremy nodded sleepily, staring at Lily as she started making some pancakes. Amanda figured he probably had never seen an Indian woman before. There probably weren't too many living in New York.

"You didn't need to get up so early," she told him, touching his arm with a pat.

They both heard footprints walking behind them, and Craig entered the kitchen through a door that led to the outside.

"You're both up early," Craig said when he saw them, as he hung his black cowboy hat on a peg obviously meant for that purpose.

"I got up to make breakfast, but Lily beat me to it," Amanda explained. She smiled at Craig and blushed as she remembered the night before, realizing that her heart had chosen her new husband.

Craig smiled back, letting her know he knew where her thoughts were. He leaned over to give Amanda a soft kiss good morning.

"I got up, so I could do my chores. I figured I had better get up early, so I can get them all done. I need you to tell me what you want done," Jeremy said.

Craig and Amanda looked at each other, and Craig sat down at the table.

"Jeremy, it's true you will have some chores around here. It is good to learn how to work. In fact, I plan to pay you for some of the work you do, but you will be doing other things too. School is almost out for the summer, but you will be going to school in the fall, when it starts up again."

"I get to go to school?" Jeremy asked, as if he didn't quite believe his good fortune.

Craig nodded. "You will also have time to do fun things," Craig explained.

"Fun things, like what?" Jeremy asked, this time with interest.

"Have you ever gone fishing?" Jeremy shook his head. "There is a pond and a river close by that are full of fish. I can teach you how to fish. You can also swim in the pond, and I can teach you how to swim if you don't know how. After school starts, you'll make friends, and you will have time to do things with them."

"Wow, I am going to like it here better than I thought," Jeremy shouted with glee.

"I have a question for you, Jeremy." Amanda looked over her shoulder to see if they had time before breakfast was ready to have this conversation and saw that they did. The bacon was done, but Lily was still working on the stack of pancakes.

"How did your sister hurt her leg?"

Jeremy slumped in his chair and was quiet for a few moments. "We were going to town, Ma, Pa, Grace, and me. Something spooked the horses, and it had started to rain hard. They started running, and Pa couldn't control them. The wagon flipped over into a gully that had water in it. Pa and Ma were pinned under the wagon in the water. I guess they drowned. I was thrown clear, so I wasn't hurt too bad. Grace was pinned under the wagon too, since Ma had been holding her, but she lived because her head wasn't under the water."

"I'm so sorry you had to go through all that, son," Craig told him, putting a hand on his shoulder in sympathy.

Jeremy wiped some tears away and looked up. "I don't remember much. I got hit on the head, and it knocked me out. It was a while before someone came to help us. Ma and Pa were dead by then. Grace was crying. We never saw Ma and Pa again. I don't know where the people buried them. They took Grace and me to a doctor. He put a bandage on my head because it was bleeding." Jeremy stopped talking long enough to lift his brown hair up off his forehead and showed them an angry-looking, jagged scar at the top on the right.

"The doctor said Grace broke her leg, but he couldn't do anything about it. He just wrapped it up. We were both taken to the orphanage. We were together for a while at that orphanage, but then we were moved to another one. They wouldn't let us be together.

"Grace couldn't walk on her leg for a long time, and then she started to try, but I think it hurts her some, because she doesn't try a lot."

"Thanks for telling us, Jeremy," Amanda told him. "I am sure that was hard to think about and remember."

"Breakfast ready," Lily said, as she placed plates of bacon, eggs, and pancakes on the table. Soon they were all eating and enjoying the good food. Amanda made sure to set some food aside for Grace when she woke up.

After breakfast, Craig asked Jeremy to get dressed, so he could take him to the barn and show him some chores that he could do.

"What an awful experience those two have had, losing their parents like that in an accident," Amanda said to Craig after Jeremy had left.

Craig looked at her. "I bet Grace's leg just wasn't set right. I think the doctor that treated them just didn't want to do anything about it because they were orphans, and there would have been no money to pay him." He slammed his fist on the table.

"Why would someone not treat a child?" Amanda wondered with anger and frustration in her voice.

"That scar Jeremy showed us on his forehead? It looks like it should have been stitched but wasn't. Those kids didn't get the care they should have gotten."

"Do you think we can do anything about it now?" Amanda wondered.

"I think we should take Grace to Dr. Collins in town and get his opinion. Maybe there is something he could do, or he would know a doctor that could."

"That's a great idea," Amanda said enthusiastically. She watched as Craig finished the last of his pancakes. "What should we do today? Is there anything I need to do?"

"Today is Saturday," Craig answered. "Let's use this day to let the children rest and let them get used to us. We can spend time together as a new family. Tomorrow we can all go to church, and Monday morning we'll take both kids to Dr. Collins for checkups and for his opinion about Grace's leg."

And that is what they did. It was a great day for each of them. Craig took Jeremy to the barn to show him how to do some simple chores, and Shep followed them around. Jeremy showed a lot of interest learning how to care for the horses. Amanda spent time with Grace, reading to her out of the new book she had picked out, and playing simple games with her.

After lunch and after Grace had rested, Craig took all three of them to the pond he had told them about. They were able to walk, as it wasn't too far away from the barn. Craig and Amanda sat by the pond and talked and enjoyed getting to know each other, while Jeremy and Grace played nearby.

Craig told Amanda about his childhood. He told her how he never knew his mother. His father was a drunk, and although he never beat Craig, he didn't take care of him very well. There were days when his father was sober, and he would work at a nearby farm or ranch for some money, but those dry spells didn't last very long. When Craig was fifteen, he was tired of living that kind of life, and he ran away, joining a cattle drive. He told Amanda how he spent the next fifteen years working at various ranches all over Texas and the surrounding states. He talked about how he saved up his money. A few years ago he was finally able to purchase this farm, as the previous owners had sold it for lower than it was really worth because they were so anxious to go to Oregon.

Craig then asked Amanda about her childhood and her marriage to David. She briefly told him about her stepfather, how hard he worked her mother and her, and that she believed her mother finally died of exhaustion when Amanda was sixteen. She then told him the story of how she met David and her eventual marriage to him.

When the children were tired of playing by the pond, they went back to the house. After dinner, Amanda read to her new family out of a book she had brought, and then she put the children to bed. Later, Craig and Amanda enjoyed more time together.

Chapter 11

THE NEXT DAY, THE FAMILY went to church. Amanda was glad that Craig took them and went into the church building with them. She had always gone to church faithfully every week, but she had never seen Craig there. He seemed comfortable though, like he had been in church before.

Reverend Watson gave a great sermon on taking care of the orphans and the poor, which Amanda felt was a fitting subject since quite a few of their town had taken children in. After church, they lingered for a while. Amanda was able to talk to her friend, Lydia, and some of the other women.

Amanda learned that Lydia and her husband, Clinton, had ended up taking two boys who were brothers, even though they had originally planned to adopt a baby or toddler. When Amanda was introduced to the boys, she could tell that they were happy with their new parents. Clinton was also happy with them, already acting like a proud father, as he told a story of giving the boys their first horse-riding lesson, and how well they did.

Lydia expressed surprise at the sudden wedding, but she then commented, "It's about time. You two are perfect for each other. I was wondering how long you would keep rejecting Craig's proposals. He was sure patient with you," she teased.

"It seems as if the entire town knew about his proposals, even though I tried to stop them," Amanda commented with embarrassment.

While they were talking, Grace had stayed next to her side, but Amanda noticed that Jeremy was talking to one of Lydia's boys, Joseph. After questioning them, she learned they were friends in the orphanage and were the same age. Amanda was glad to see Jeremy had a friend. She and Lydia made plans to get the boys together soon.

MONDAY MORNING WAS chaotic. Grace, for the first time, showed reluctance to walk at all. She wanted to be carried everywhere. Amanda didn't know if she was insisting to be carried, because she knew someone would, or if her leg really did hurt. Jeremy was not happy about having to go to the doctor and took off running, when he was told of the plans. Craig let him run, but when he could see the boy was running too far and getting close to the field with a large bull in it, he went after him on a horse.

Eventually, they were all in the wagon on their way to town. Craig gave Jeremy a good talking to about running away and how dangerous that was on a farm, where he was not familiar with places and animals he needed to avoid. Amanda held Grace close to her, as she whimpered all the way into town, responding to the tension from her brother.

When they finally arrived in front of the doctor's office, Craig jumped down from the wagon and went inside to make sure the doctor was there and willing to see them. He came back out with the doctor's wife, Mrs. Pamela Collins.

"Why don't you and Grace come inside, while the doctor spends time with Jeremy," Mrs. Collins suggested to Amanda.

She thought it was a good idea. After Craig helped her down from the wagon and placed Grace into her arms, she followed Pamela into her home.

"Would you like some milk and cookies?" Mrs. Collins asked Grace who hid her face on Amanda's shoulder, but nodded her agreement for the treat. They went to the kitchen, where an older girl sat at the table reading a book.

"Deborah, we have company." Mrs. Collins spoke to the girl and introduced Amanda and Grace.

Deborah smiled shyly at them and then said, "It's nice to meet you, ma'am. Hello, Grace."

"You must be one of the children from the orphan train," Amanda said to Deborah. "Welcome to Maple Grove."

The adults talked for a while, including both girls in the conversation when they could. Grace had just finished her milk and cookies, when Craig walked in with a much calmer Jeremy.

"The doctor can see Grace now," Craig turned to Mrs. Collins. "Could Jeremy stay here with you while Amanda and I take Grace to see Dr. Collins?"

"Of course," Mrs. Collins replied. "I'm sure he would like some milk and cookies."

Craig picked up Grace and guided Amanda into the office Dr. Collins had on the side of their house.

"Jeremy seems to be doing better," Amanda remarked on the way.

"Yes," Craig agreed. "He discovered that Dr. Collins is much kinder than the other doctors he has been in contact with."

When they entered the office, Dr. Collins greeted Amanda and then Grace.

"This is Dr. Collins, Grace." Amanda explained to her. "We would like him to look at your leg. Would you be able to let him do that?"

Grace nodded her head, but she climbed onto Amanda's lap and wrapped her arms around Amanda's neck. Grace would not let go of her neck, so she could set her down.

"I'll just look at it while you sit on your mother's lap, how's that?" Dr. Collins asked Grace.

Amanda took off Grace's shoe and stocking and watched as the doctor looked over her leg very thoroughly. He pressed in certain areas and rubbed on others. Grace was quiet through the examination, until the doctor tried to straighten part of her leg. Then she cried out in pain and tried to pull her leg away from the doctor.

Dr. Collins looked at Craig. "You can take her back to Pamela now, and she can watch both children. I would like to talk to you both privately."

When Craig returned, Dr. Collins sat down across from both of them.

"Let's talk about Jeremy first. He's about as healthy as a child can be despite having spent the last few years in an orphanage. He is a mite thin, but that will improve, I'm sure, with good food and freedom outside."

Craig looked relieved at this news. "What about the scar on his forehead?"

The doctor nodded. "I do agree that it probably should have been stitched, but there's not much we can do about it now. It doesn't seem to bother him, and, if he keeps his hair a little longer in the front, it shouldn't be noticeable to others."

"What about Grace's leg, doctor?" Amanda asked. "It seems to cause her pain, and she will barely walk on it."

The doctor looked at her with concern. "Craig told me what happened to her leg. It should have been set. If it had been set properly, it wouldn't even be bothering her now."

"It is so hard for me to think a doctor would refuse to treat a child properly," Amanda said with grief for her daughter.

"I agree. I have some bad news, but I also have some possible good news. I can't do anything for Grace. I don't have the skills or the equipment. But, I do know of a doctor who is located in the city who might be able to help her. It would mean surgery, possibly more than one, re-breaking the bone and casting it to heal properly. It would also mean some intense therapy afterward He might not be able to make the leg like new, but he should be able to fix it enough that she will only walk with a slight limp with little or no pain."

"That's great news. When do you think we can have this done?" Amanda asked with a smile.

"I will give you a letter you can take to the doctor. You can go to the city for an initial appointment whenever you are ready."

"I am so relieved," Amanda turned to Craig with joy in her eyes. "I was so worried she would never be able to walk without pain." She did not recognize that Craig was not showing as much as joy as she was. "We should make plans to go as soon as possible."

"What do we do in the meantime, doctor?" Craig asked. "Should we be making her walk?"

"I wouldn't advise that," the doctor shook his head. "If she is forced to walk on it, it could make things worse. I would let her walk when she feels she can. Children are resilient, and I doubt she will refuse to walk just because she doesn't want to. If she is refusing, it is probably because she is in pain."

"She was refusing to walk this morning," Amanda commented, "yet she walked quite a bit yesterday."

"If she walked a lot yesterday, she might have over done it and is sore today." The doctor nodded. "I am glad you want to take care of this soon. If you are willing to wait for a few minutes, I will write out that letter so you can go whenever you choose."

After the doctor left the room, Amanda continued to talk about how excited she was that there was something that could be done for Grace. After a few minutes, she realized Craig did not seem as excited.

"Is something wrong?" Amanda asked him.

"This is going to cost quite a bit. I won't have the money to pay for it until after the crops are in this fall."

"Oh, money isn't a problem." Amanda waved her hand, as if she was brushing the concern away. "I have more than enough to pay for it."

Craig became very silent. "What do you mean, you have enough?"

"My late husband inherited some money which became mine when he died," Amanda explained, not understanding why he was upset. "I have hardly used any of it. I am so glad I didn't because now I can use it to help Grace."

"How much do you have?" Craig asked.

Amanda named an amount.

"You have enough that you didn't need to work. I thought you had to work, and that's why you had your sewing shop," Craig commented.

"I started my dress shop because I needed something to keep me busy, and I enjoyed it," Amanda replied.

"Well, I consider that money yours. We are married now, and it is my responsibility to take care of this family and earn the money for any expenses. I don't want to use any of your money," Craig said sharply.

"I don't understand," Amanda said with confusion in her eyes. "We are married, which means we share everything. My money is now our money and can be used for things the children need or for anything else for that matter."

"It is the man's job to provide for his family, and that is what I will do," Craig said firmly. "I should have enough money by fall to pay for the operation. We will need to wait until then."

"Do you mean that, even though we have this opportunity and the means to fix Grace's leg, you want her to wait for several months because you are insisting on paying for it?" Amanda questioned him. "You are willing to make Grace keep dealing with her pain? That doesn't seem quite right."

"It is what will happen. I don't appreciate your hiding the fact that you have money," Craig said, as he stood up and started to walk out of the office. "I don't want to talk about it anymore. I am going to get the kids, and we will wait for you in the wagon. You go ahead and wait for the letter."

Amanda sat in her chair, stunned at what had just happened. It just did not make sense to her. Why would he make Grace live with pain for three or four more months, because he wanted to pay for it? It never occurred to her to tell Craig about her money. She was not trying to hide it from him. The money really did not matter to her. She was glad she now had a chance to use it for some good.

The doctor soon came in and gave her the letter. Amanda left as soon as she could after promising Dr. Collins that they would keep him up to date. She did not say anything to him about her argument with Craig, and she let him continue to believe they were going to take Grace to the city as soon as possible.

Chapter 12

THERE WERE A LOT OF adjustments in the next few weeks, but Jeremy and Grace surprisingly did very well, considering all the major changes in their lives.

Jeremy followed his new dad around like a little puppy. Wherever Craig went, Jeremy was not far behind. He learned how to care for the horses, and Craig told Amanda one day during the evening meal that Jeremy had a gift with horses.

"Even Apache, who is known to kick for no reason, is calm around Jeremy," Craig bragged. "In fact, I have an idea." He looked at Jeremy, as he pushed his empty plate away.

"If you help with the crops and around the farm doing odd jobs, in the fall I will give you Apache for your very own."

"Do you mean it?" Jeremy's eyes lit up with excitement, but then he lowered them. "I don't know much about tending to the crops."

"I realize that, and I will teach you. That's my job, and, if I am doing something else, John can help teach you."

"Alright!" Jeremy exclaimed, looking like he was about ready to jump out of his seat in excitement.

Another time Amanda was sitting in one of the porch chairs sewing a new shirt for Jeremy. Grace was sitting on the stairs nearby playing with her doll. Craig walked up to Grace with a wrapped cloth bundle in his arms. He bent down and sat near Grace.

"I have a surprise for you," he said and put the bundle in her lap.

Grace carefully unwrapped it, and a little kitten's head poked through the brown cloth.

"Oh," Grace breathed, as she looked at the kitten. "For my very own?" she asked, as she could hardly believe her good fortune.

"Yes, she's yours. The barn cat had kittens, and they're old enough to leave their mother and find new homes."

"What's her name?" Grace asked, as she pulled the kitten out from the cloth. It was gray and white in color.

"You can choose, but choose a girl's name."

Grace scrunched her eyes closed for a few seconds in thought, and then announced, "I'm going to name her Emma."

Amanda heard a gasp behind her. She turned around and saw Jeremy standing there.

"That was Ma's name," he quietly explained.

Amanda looked at Craig and watched, as he sat next to Grace giving her instructions on the kitten's care. Amanda felt the stirrings of new love within her for her new husband. She more than just cared for him. She was falling in love with him.

Amanda also spent a few days a week at the dress shop. Craig had provided her with a buggy and horse, and she always took Grace with her. Amanda had quickly found a young woman, Julie, to train, and she was now doing most of the work for the shop. Amanda was finding that she was losing her desire to own a dress shop. She had only started the shop to keep her busy and because there was a need for someone to make dresses in Maple Grove.

She now wanted to be busy at the farm taking care of her new family. Amanda hoped that she could someday in the near future transfer the store to Julie. She knew Craig would be happy with that decision, since he had expressed just that morning his worry that she was taking care of too many things. He wanted her to be able to take the time to enjoy her new family.

But not everything in Amanda's new life had a silver lining. She was very concerned about Grace's leg. She could tell it hurt and bothered Grace, although she did have better days where she could walk more. Craig refused to talk about it with Amanda, although he carried Grace around whenever he could and always showed caring and concern for her.

Amanda had tried to talk the situation out with Craig a few times, and he would turn away or leave the room. Amanda got the definite message he resented the idea she had the money and means to help Grace, and he did not. Amanda started to feel that Craig was rejecting her, and she wondered if he regretted his multiple proposals now that he was stuck with her and knew about her money.

CRAIG WATCHED AS AMANDA drove away in the buggy with Grace at her side, as they headed towards town to work in her dress shop. He had noticed that there was sadness in her eyes, and he knew his reaction about her money was hurting her.

He did not know why it bothered him so much that she had more money than he did. Ever since he had been out on his own at the age of fifteen, he was proud that he was able to support himself. He had worked hard and long hours and had saved every penny he could. He had gone without needed clothing and other items and had only eaten simple foods. It had taken almost fifteen years, but he was finally able to purchase the farm he now owned, and he was proud of this accomplishment. He had succeeded further than his father ever had.

Did he resent that Amanda's money was essentially given to her? That she hadn't really worked for it or earned it? That it was inheritance money? He knew she was a hard worker. She had done well with her dress shop. She did her share helping Lily with meals and keeping the farmhouse clean. The children looked clean and well cared for. She was an excellent mother. He could tell she cared deeply for them and loved them.

He enjoyed watching Amanda as she read to Grace or played checkers with Jeremy. She was different when the children were around her, more alive and less sad. She was constantly touching them and giving them hugs, letting them know in her own way that she loved them and was glad they were in her life.

When she was alone with him, she was more formal and distant. She allowed him to hold and kiss her at night, and she seemed to enjoy the closeness, as much as he did. Yet it seemed to him she only talked to him when she needed to, and it was usually when she had questions about the children or the house.

For the first few days after the doctor's visit, she tried to talk to him about her concerns for Grace, but he always rebuffed her and would quickly walk away with an excuse that he needed to take care of a chore or an animal on the farm. She had since stopped trying to talk to him about it.

He wished the money didn't bother him so much. He wished he had known about it before he married her. He wished she hadn't kept the knowledge from him, though she adamantly denied keeping it from him on purpose.

If he had known, would he have still married her? Craig thought long and hard about that question and was able to quickly answer that, yes, he still would have married her. He suddenly realized that he loved her and was grateful circumstances made it so that she finally agreed to marry him. He missed seeing her smile that was just for him. Suddenly everything within him longed for that sight. He knew he needed to come to terms with her money. He just didn't know how to do that.

Chapter 13

THREE WEEKS AFTER THE doctor's visit, Amanda decided she had given Craig enough time to get used to the idea of her money. After the children were in bed one evening, Amanda invited Craig into the kitchen for some leftover cake and coffee.

"We need to talk about Grace," Amanda started the conversation, when they were seated across from each other.

"Why? Is something wrong?" Craig asked with concern in his voice.

"I think her leg is really bothering her," Amanda explained. "She has lived a fairly sedentary lifestyle before coming here. She probably didn't need to move around very much in the orphanage. But now that she is living on a farm, she wants to walk. She tries to, and I'm afraid she could be causing more damage to her leg."

Craig sighed. "What are you trying to say, Amanda?" His lips thinned, as if he knew the answer.

"I think we need to reconsider using the money David left me to fix her leg, now."

"You know my feelings about this," Craig fairly shouted at her. "We wait until the crops are in."

"Is it fair to make Grace wait because of your pride?" Amanda asked.

"This isn't about pride. It's about me as the head of this household supporting this family."

"And what about my role?" Amanda questioned. "Aren't we partners in this marriage? Shouldn't we be raising these children together?"

"Yes, your role is the care of the children and the house. That is a wife's role."

"Shouldn't we be sharing these roles?"

"Yes, when it's needed." While they were arguing, neither saw a shadow in the kitchen doorway.

"It will be expensive to fix Grace's leg. We need to wait until I can earn the money, and that won't happen until the crops are in." Craig stood up. "I have made this decision. I don't want to talk about it again." He left the kitchen and went outside to make his final check on the animals in the barn before bed. The shadow in the kitchen doorway slowly disappeared.

Amanda sat at the kitchen table trying to fight tears from her eyes. She had learned to love Craig. She loved how good he was to the kids. He treated both children the same, not favoring one over the other. He was a good father, and she knew his hesitation was not because he didn't love Grace and didn't want her leg fixed. She wished her money wasn't coming between them in their marriage.

I'll just have to really watch Grace and do my best to keep her quiet until she can have the surgery in the fall, Amanda thought. *When this is all over, I am going to divide the money and put it in a trust fund for the children. That way it will no longer be my money, but it will be Jeremy's and Grace's money. Maybe Craig will feel better about it then.*

JEREMY CREPT SLOWLY back to his bed. He had gotten up because he was thirsty and wanted a drink of water. He heard Amanda and Craig talking in the kitchen and heard Grace's name, so he stood in the hallway to listen. What he heard scared him. He heard his new parents talking about her leg, how bad it was, and how expensive it would be to fix, so they had to wait a long time until they earned the money.

Jeremy crept back to his bed, crawled in under the covers, and curled up into a ball. He knew it cost a lot of money to adopt them. Craig and Amanda had spent a lot of money the day they agreed to be his and Grace's parents. He felt really bad and knew he needed to do something. Maybe he could help tons around the farm, get up early when his new dad did, and work until the sun went down. Maybe that would help. Jeremy thought about the money Craig was giving him for the little work he had done around the farm. It wasn't much, but maybe it would be enough to help Grace, at least a little bit.

Then suddenly Jeremy knew what he needed to do. He did not want to be a burden on this new family. He loved it here on the farm and really wanted to stay, but maybe, if he used his money he had earned, got on the train, and went back to the orphanage, there would be extra money to get Grace's leg fixed. They could take the clothes that were purchased for him and his harmonica back to the store. They would only need to feed Grace. That could give them extra money to get Grace's leg fixed.

THE NEXT MORNING, AMANDA woke up right after Craig left their bed to start the day. She washed her face with the water that was sitting on the bureau in a large bowl and brushed her hair. She braided it and rolled it up into her usual bun in the back of her head. She put on a yellow and blue-flowered dress and left her room.

She opened Jeremy's bedroom door quietly and peeked inside. She could see that he was still asleep, buried under his covers like usual. Amanda chuckled to herself. She didn't know how he could sleep under blankets that way since it had been so hot lately. She next checked Grace's room and saw that she was also quietly sleeping, with her curly, blond hair spread out all over her pillow. Grace's new kitten was curled up at the foot of her bed and lifted her head up briefly to see who had disturbed her sleep.

She walked down the stairs and entered the kitchen to help Lily get breakfast ready.

"Good morning," Amanda greeted Lily.

"Good morning, Mrs. Parker," Lily repeated. "We get rain today, maybe. Good for crops."

"Yes, it would be nice to get a rainstorm. It should cool things off a bit, too. It's been so hot this week," Amanda replied.

Both women worked together frying bacon, making pancakes, and scrambled eggs, talking together as they worked.

Amanda looked at the clock and knew Craig and John would be coming in soon for the morning meal. She promised herself that she would greet Craig as if she wasn't angry. She remembered her promise to herself to make sure Grace didn't walk too much. She stopped and listened carefully to the floor above, making sure she didn't hear any little footsteps. Grace had tried to leave her room and go down the stairs on her own before.

All of a sudden Craig rushed in. "Where's Jeremy?" he demanded the women.

"Why, he's up in his bed I checked on him before I came down to help fix breakfast," Amanda said.

"Apache is missing. I can't find him anywhere. He was there last night when I checked the animals."

"Could someone have stolen him?" Amanda wondered.

"I doubt it. If someone wanted to take him, they would have likely taken the other horses as well."

Both Amanda and Craig looked at each other, both coming to the same horrible conclusion together.

"Jeremy!" They both yelled, as they raced up the stairs. Craig beat her to Jeremy's room first, and he ran inside.

"See, he is under the covers asleep, just like I saw him, when I checked on him earlier," Amanda explained pointing to the mound on the bed, but Craig walked over and pulled the covers off the bed. There lay a rolled-up blanket and pillows instead of Jeremy.

"Make sure Grace is still in her bed," Craig ordered, as he left the room to see for himself.

They both ran into Grace's room, and she was sitting up in bed rubbing her eyes sleepily. "Is it breakfast time?" she asked them.

"In a little while," Craig answered. "Do you know where Jeremy is?"

Grace shook her head and started to climb out of bed. "I'll help find him."

Amanda stopped her. "Let's get you dressed first. Maybe Daddy will find him, before we're done." She tried to speak as calmly as she could, but she looked at Craig, and her eyes were frightened.

"Maybe he is in the barn or somewhere around the farm, and I just didn't see him," Craig said, as he rushed out of Grace's room. "I'll go look around."

Amanda helped Grace dress quickly and carried her down to the kitchen.

"Lily will give you something to eat," Amanda told Grace. "I am going to see if they found Jeremy yet."

"I want Jeremy to eat with me," Grace whined.

"We'll find him soon, and then he can eat with you." Amanda looked at Lily. "Can you watch her for me?"

"Yes, we eat breakfast together," Lily smiled at Grace, then looked at Amanda with concern in her eyes. "John looking for Jeremy, too."

Amanda nodded her appreciation and ran outside. She could not see Craig or John. She called Jeremy's and Craig's name a few times; then she gave up and returned to the house. She had an awful feeling inside, like something was very wrong. It wasn't like Jeremy to just disappear like this. Where would he go?

Amanda went back upstairs into Jeremy's room looking for clues. She looked at the table next to his bed and saw the cup that had held Jeremy's few coins he had earned was tipped over, and the money was gone. It looked like he had indeed run away.

Then she saw the paper. It was on the floor halfway hidden under Jeremy's bed. It looked like it had writing on it. She picked it up and read, "I am going to go back to the orphanage. Take care of Grace for me."

Clutching the paper, Amanda ran down the stairs and back outside, yelling for Craig as she did. She ran to the barn and right up to Craig, as he swung himself on top of a horse.

"I found a note," she explained breathlessly and thrust it at him. He read it quickly and then handed it back. "Where did he get the idea we didn't want him? Why would he want to go back to the orphanage?" Amanda asked.

"We need to find him to get those answers," Craig said. "Maybe he went to town, to the train station. I'll head there now."

"I want to go with you," Amanda demanded. Craig looked like he was going to refuse, but she looked at him deep in his eyes. "He is my son, too."

Craig nodded his agreement that she could come. "Get on the horse that I saddled for John." Craig got off his horse, went to talk to John for a moment, then came over and started to help Amanda onto the horse's back. Before he lifted her up, they looked at each other for a moment. He quickly gave her a strong hug and wiped the tears from her eyes. "We'll find him Amanda, don't worry."

She nodded her head and allowed Craig to help her onto the horse. They were both soon riding towards Maple Grove.

Chapter 14

AMANDA AND CRAIG RODE to the train station as fast as they could. When they got there, they did not see a train, but they immediately saw the missing Apache, his reins tied to a post, and a little boy sitting on a bench nearby.

Amanda pointed, "There he is!"

Amanda got off her horse by herself and ran over to Jeremy and hugged him. "We have been looking all over for you," she exclaimed, wiping tears from her eyes. "Why would you want to leave? I thought you were happy living with us."

Craig sat down on the bench next to Jeremy. The boy looked down at his shoes and didn't say anything.

"We need to know the reason, so we can fix it," Craig told him.

"I heard you guys arguing last night about Grace's leg," Jeremy finally said. "You don't have the money to fix it, and the surgery will have to wait until you can get the money. I figured, if I left and went back to the orphanage, you could use the money you spend on me and could get her leg fixed sooner. You could sell the clothes you bought me and the harmonica. You would only have to feed Grace, and so you could save that money, too."

"You were going to go all the way to New York by yourself?" Amanda asked. "Don't you know how dangerous that would be?"

"How were you going to pay for the train?" Craig asked the boy. Jeremy opened his fist and showed them the few coins he had earned. "I was going to use this, but the station master said it wasn't enough." He reached over and placed the coins into Craig's hand "Maybe you can use this money to help get Grace's leg fixed."

"Oh, Jeremy," Amanda hugged him again. "If only you had talked to us instead of running away."

"Running away doesn't solve problems, son," Craig said. Then his eyes widened with recognition, as he realized that was what he was doing, running from Amanda instead of being willing to talk to her about the money and working out a solution together. He looked at Amanda with an apology in his eyes.

"I didn't think to talk to you about it," Jeremy admitted. "I heard you say you didn't want to talk about it anymore." He looked at Craig, as he said this.

"Well, I was wrong." Craig looked at Amanda, hoping she would understand what he was trying to say. "We are a family now, all four of us. We need to work out our problems and concerns together."

Amanda smiled at Craig and then looked at Jeremy. "We will be getting Grace's leg fixed. We just need to wait until the fall. You can help us by keeping Grace from walking too much and..."

"No," Craig interrupted, as he made an instant decision. "Did you know that your new mom is a widow, Jeremy?" The boy shook his head. "Well, when her first husband died, he had a lot of money, and he left it to her. She wants to use some of that money to get Grace's leg fixed. What do you think about that?"

"Truly?" Jeremy looked at Amanda hopefully. "We can get her leg fixed, and I can still stay with you?"

"Yes," Amanda agreed joyfully and threw her arms around Craig. Then she turned to her son. "But Jeremy, even if we didn't have that money, we still want you with us. You are an important part of our family. Please promise us you will never run away again."

Jeremy promised them both. After a few more hugs and wiping away tears, they got on their horses and started on their way back to their farm.

When they arrived at the farm, Lily ran out of the house and started to fuss over Jeremy, insisting he come inside and eat a huge breakfast. She led him inside the house. Craig took the reins of all three horses and walked to the barn to take care of them. Amanda followed him inside.

"Did you mean what you told Jeremy?" Amanda asked him.

"Yes, I did," Craig answered her, as he began to remove a saddle from one of the horses. "While Jeremy was talking, I began to see I was letting my pride in taking care of my family get in the way of what was really important, getting Grace's leg fixed." He swung the saddle into its place on a stable wall, then turned to Amanda and pulled her close to him.

"What you said last night is true. We are partners in this marriage. I have had a hard time thinking that you had a better life with your first husband. I can't provide for you like he could have."

"It's true that I did have a good life with David. I loved him very much." Amanda reached up to touch his face. "But I have a good life here, too. The money he left me means nothing to me. In fact, I believe that God wants us to use it for Grace, and, if there is anything left over, we can use it for the children's education. I will agree to just use it, if we need it for the children. I will allow you to provide for me as my husband."

These were the words that Craig wanted to hear, and he crushed her to him. He felt so grateful that she was his wife. "I love you," he told her and then kissed her in a way that told her of his love for her. As he kissed her, Amanda realized that, before she had married Craig, she had been buried in the past, believing she would never love again. Craig had shown her differently.

"Oh, Craig, I love you, too." Amanda kissed him back.

4 Weeks Later

AMANDA AND CRAIG WERE sitting in the hospital room beside Grace's bed, while she slept. The doctor had just left the room after telling them that the surgery had gone well. After her leg healed from the surgery, she should be able to walk with only a slight limp and with little or no pain. Grace would be in the hospital for several days and would need to exercise and strengthen her leg, but Amanda planned on learning how to do the exercises for Grace, so they could do them at home.

"I am so glad that the surgery is over, and it went well," Amanda said, as she reached over to hold Craig's hand.

"So am I," Craig agreed. "I am glad we did the surgery now. From what the doctor said, it wouldn't have been a good idea to wait until fall."

"I have some news for you," Amanda smiled at him. "How would you like to have a larger family?"

"What do you mean? Do you want to adopt another child?" Craig questioned her.

"No, I think this would happen the natural way." She waited to see if Craig figured out what she meant.

As her words sunk in, his face lit up. "Are you going to have a child?"

"Yes, probably sometime early next spring," Amanda confirmed. "I wasn't sure how you would feel about it. We have never talked about more children. I didn't think I could have children since I was married so long to David and never became pregnant."

"I love the idea of more children." Craig pulled Amanda close. "After all, we have all those rooms in the house to fill."

For the latest information on updates, new releases and sales for Zoe Matthews' books, you can sign up for her newsletter at www.zoematthewsromances.com[1]. You will also receive three free books!!!!

1. http://www.zoematthewsromances.com

Sneak Peek to

"The Promise of a Family"

Lydia Brown walked up the stairs from the kitchen to go to her father's bedroom. He had requested that she come speak with him right after lunch. He had been sick in bed for the last few weeks, but he was not getting better. He had been slowly wasting away for the last month and was starting to complain about pain in his abdomen. Lydia had been praying fervently that her father would get well and be able to work with her again in their tailor shop. Lydia had been working in their shop, since she finished school when she was 16 years old, and she treasured the times working with her father.

As Lydia knocked on her father's bedroom door, she hoped one of the subjects her father wanted to talk about was giving his permission for her to finally marry Richard Smith, the son of a local banker in Chicago where they lived. Richard had asked her to marry him when she was 18, and her father had refused to give permission, saying that he wanted her to wait until she was 20 years old. She could not get him to give any other reason than that. Even though she obeyed him, she wished he had given his permission. Many of her friends from school had married, and some of them already had their first child.

She knocked on the door and heard her father weakly tell her to enter. She walked into the darkened room. In a split second, she could tell that he was not doing well. His face looked gray, and even though he tried to raise his arm in greeting, he could barely lift his hand. This was not what Lydia wanted to see. She did her best to fight the tears that threatened to come, as she forced a smile on her face as she greeted him.

"Hello, Father." She bent down to kiss his cheek.

"Hello, Lydia," he weakly replied. "Sit here by my side. I have much to discuss with you."

Lydia did as he bid and sat down on a wooden chair that had been placed next to his bed.

"I have a story to tell you," her father said slowly. "And while I tell you, I must ask you to listen to what I have to say until I am done."

"I don't want you to tax yourself, Father," Lydia objected, as she reached to take his hand. "Maybe you should rest, and we can talk later."

"No!" he exclaimed, as forcefully as he could in his weakened state. "I must tell you now. If I wait, it may be too late." He took a deep breath. "You do realize I am dying, don't you?"

Lydia reluctantly nodded, and this time she allowed her tears to fall. "I was hoping the new medicine the doctor gave you to try a few days ago would help."

"It's too late," her father shook his head. "I must tell you why your mother and I were able to come to America."

Lydia felt confused. "I've heard this story many times, papa."

"You haven't heard the whole story."

"Okay, I will listen to what you have to say."

"When your mother and I lived in England, I was the valet for the son of a lord. You know what a valet is, don't you?"

"Yes, someone who took care of the clothes and needs of a privileged person."

"Good," her father continued his story. "This son's name was George Byron. He and I were actually good friends. We grew up together, and, although my duties were to take care of his clothes and appearance, he never treated me as a servant. George was educated by tutors, and I was allowed to sit in on the lessons. When he was old enough to attend boarding school, I went with him. Although I couldn't attend his classes, he would teach me things that he had learned in the evenings.

"When he was an adult and had graduated from college, he married. Since he was the youngest son of his family, he wasn't going to inherit any land or property. All of that went to his oldest brother. He did receive some inheritance money when he was of age, so he decided he would take that money and his new wife and immigrate to America."

Her father paused and tried to reach for a glass of water that sat nearby on a table. Lydia helped him get a drink. He then continued.

"George and his wife settled in a town called Maple Grove, Texas. He purchased a cattle ranch with part of his inheritance money. He hired a man who lived there to be his foreman and teach him all about cattle ranching.

"A few years after George came to America, he wrote to me and offered to pay for your mother's and my expenses to come to America. He wanted us to settle in Texas, but I wanted to open a tailor shop. So he lent me the money to bring us to America and then here to Chicago to start our shop."

"That was very nice of him," Lydia commented.

"Yes, it was. We would not have been able to come here otherwise. So your mother and I came to America, to Chicago. We opened up the tailor shop and were able to purchase this home. Then you were born. I insisted on paying him back the money. At first, he wouldn't hear of it. He finally agreed, but he allowed me to pay it back at my leisure. I insisted on a due date when it all needed to be paid back. We finally agreed..."

Lydia's father paused, as if he had something hard to say, and he did not want to say it.

"It's okay," Lydia encouraged him. She was now curious and wanted to know the ending. "Just tell me."

He took a deep breath. "We agreed that I would have the money paid back by the time you turned 20 years old."

Lydia was confused. "What did I have to do with this?" Then she had a terrible thought. "Have you been able to pay it back?"

Her father continued, as if she hadn't spoken. "Once the tailor shop was open and making a profit, I was able to pay a little of the money back every year. But things haven't been going as well as I had hoped with our shop, not since that larger, clothing store opened up down the street."

Lydia knew what her father was talking about. A few years ago, a large, clothing store for men opened up a few blocks away from their store. They offered not only high-quality clothing but also offered tailoring services right in their building. Since that store opened, customers that used to frequent her father's shop started going to the larger one. It was easier to purchase clothing and have them fitted in the same place. The only customers they regularly had now were some loyal men who had been coming to their shop, since it had opened almost 20 years ago.

"I have had to take out a loan against our shop, Lydia." Her father wheezed and stopped talking again for a drink of water. After a few swallows, he continued. "I have not been able to pay George back all of his money, nor pay back the bank."

Lydia sat back in her chair in disbelief. She knew there were problems financially, but she had not known how bad. "Why didn't you tell me this before now? I could have helped in some way."

"I didn't want you to worry, and I thought I would be able to pay off the loans. But then I got sick."

"So what are we going to do?"

"I'm not done with my story yet. Please listen. What I have to say will not be easy for me to tell, or for you to hear."

Lydia nodded apprehensively and hoped what he had to say would not be too awful and that she would be able to figure out a way to get them out of this mess.

"I made an agreement with my friend, George Byron. We agreed that, if I was not able to pay back his loan by the time you were 20-years old, you would marry his son."

Lydia gasped at his words and started to protest. He held up a hand to keep her from talking and continued. "George has a son who is four-years older than you. His name is Clinton. Regrettably, George died two years ago, but even though he is no longer around, I must honor my promise to him. I cannot pay back the loan to George. I cannot pay back the loan to the bank. When I die, the bank will be taking over the store and this house. You will not have anywhere to go. You must go to Texas and marry Clinton."

"Father, I can't do that," Lydia protested. "I don't even know the man. How do you know that he will be good to me? You haven't seen Mr. Byron in years. How do you know this will be something that will work out with his son?"

"I knew George very well. He was my best friend, my comrade. He never treated me like a servant, even though I was one. He treated me like a friend. He has raised his son well. I am confident his son will treat you well."

"But he doesn't even know me. Why would he want to marry a woman he has never met? And what about Richard?" Lydia reminded her father. "Richard wants to marry me. Is this why you would not give me permission to marry Richard?"

"Yes," her father admitted. "The loan is due in full on the day you turn 20, which is in a few months. I couldn't agree to a marriage to someone else, until I had satisfied this loan with George."

"I want to marry Richard, Father," Lydia argued. "I love him. I don't want to be forced to marry a man I have never met."

"Richard will not be a good husband to you. He will not treat you as you deserve to be treated. I think you know this deep down inside. His father is the one who will be taking over the shop and this home. There is a reason why Richard has been courting you."

At her father's words, she remembered a conversation a few days ago with Richard, where he had grabbed her arm in anger, because she had refused to leave her father's bedside and go on a walk with him.

There had been some other instances in the past few months that had concerned her as well, but she had always excused Richard, telling herself he was tired, or he had been working hard. She knew deep down, her father was right to be concerned about Richard.

"I want you to listen to me very carefully. I must give you some instructions." Her father's voice was weakening. Lydia again took her father's hand and encouraged him to continue.

"I have purchased a train ticket for you to go to Maple Grove, Texas. I have also set aside some money that you can use to purchase things that you will need and for food when you travel. I have hidden these items in my desk, in the hidden compartment. I have included instructions on sending a telegram to Mr. Clinton Bryon and his address, so you can let him know you are coming. He is aware that you might be coming soon.

"After I am gone...."

Lydia tried to protest again at his words, but he cut her off. "After I am gone, after the funeral, I want you to leave for Maple Grove immediately, the very next day. If the bank finds that ticket and money before you are able to leave, you will then find you have no other choice. I am giving you a chance to have a good life. I am confident you will have a good life with Clinton.

"You are to tell no one what your plans are, except Noreen." He named the woman who had helped care for Lydia since her mother died ten years ago and now was nursing her father. "She knows of this plan, and she will help you get to the station when it is time.

"You have always been an obedient daughter. I have been blessed to be your father. I am asking you to honor my wishes this last time. Will you do this?"

Go to www.zoematthewsromances.com[1] for information on how to purchase this book.

---

1.   http://www.zoematthewsromances.com

Please check out Zoe Matthews'social media sites!!

Website: www.zoematthewsromances.com[2]

Facebook: https://www.facebook.com/zoematthewssr/

Twitter: https://twitter.com/ZoeMatthewsSR

Instagram: https://www.instagram.com/zoematthewssr/

Amazon Author Page: https://www.amazon.com/Zoe-Matthews/ e/B00LDT94U4/ ref=la_B00LDT94U4_ntt_srch_lnk_1?qid=1526408961&sr=1-1

Email Address: Zoe@zoematthewsromances.com

---

2. http://www.zoematthewsromances.com

Also by Zoe Matthews

Have you read these books?

The Orphan Train Romance Series
In the late 1800s, many orphans were sent to different states in the western United States in order to be provided with stable and loving homes. This series features fictitious orphans who traveled to Texas, the families with which they found homes, and the love they found when they were adults.

An Unexpected Family

The Promise of a Family

Anna

Serena

Katrina

Westward Promises

Westward Skies

Orphan Train Romance Series Boxset, Books 1-5

Majestic Mountain Ranch Romance Series
Six siblings come together at their family ranch after their father's death. They work together to convert their ranch into a dude ranch. Along the way, each of them finds true love.

Colorado Dreams

Colorado Secrets

Colorado Destiny

Colorado Dawn

Colorado Skies

Colorado Promises

Colorado Christmas

Majestic Mountain Ranch Series Boxset, Books 1-7

Mail-Order Brides of America Series

After the death of their infant daughter, Mary, Elizabeth and Thomas decide to open their large plantation home to orphan girls who need a second chance. They name their new home "Mary's Home for Girls." Each book features one of these girls, how they came to Mary's Home, and the decision they make as adults to become a mail-order bride.

Each book is set in a different state.

Southern Belle, Prequel

Iowa Destiny

Texas Hearts

Montana Legacy

Nebraska Promise

South Dakota Jewel

Mail-Order Brides of America Series, Five Books in One!

Time Travel Romance Series

Written by Zoe Matthews and Jade Jenson, a mother/daughter team This series is based in modern times, as well as in the 1800s. Nicki and her friends find themselves swept up in the past when Nicki reads an ad in her local newspaper, advertising for a mail-order bride. Curious, she answers the ad and is soon sent back in time to meet Patrick, a man who owns a large ranch deep in the Rocky Mountains, and his siblings. Nicki's friends soon become involved and what happens next changes their lives forever.

Touched by Time

River of Time

Winds of Time
Time Travel Romance Boxset, Books 1-3
Secrets of Time
Changed by Time
Christmas in Time
Time Travel Romance Boxset, Books 4-6
Time Travel Romance Boxset, Books 1-6

Harvey Girls Romance Series

Written by Zoe Matthews and Evelyn Michaels, a mother/daughter team
Adelia Burke has co-authored books 4 and beyond
Follow a large family of men (and one daughter) who live in Arizona near the Grand Canyon at the beginning of the 1900s. This series is Historical fiction about the Harvey Girls, a true event that was started by a man named Fred Harvey. These women helped shaped the West in their own way, just as much as the men did.

Desert Dreams
Desert Wishes
Desert Bells
Harvey Girls Romance Series Boxset, Books 1-3
Desert Lily
Desert Sky
Desert Star (coming soon)

Millennial Mail-Order Brides Romance Series

Daniel has six grandchildren who refuse to marry and settle down. So he has to take matters into his own hands. He signs each of them up with a dating website and matches them with someone of his choosing. But will his grandchildren cooperate and allow him to be a modern-day matchmaker?

Always and Forever

Now and Forever

A New Love

A Forever Dream

You're My Everything

Lead Me with Your Heart

Millennial Mail-Order Brides Romance Boxset, Books 1-6

Time Travel Guardians Romance Series

It is 2045 and time travel has been proven to be real. But many devices are falling into the wrong hands, so the Time Travel Guardians were born. Their job is to use time travel to find each device before they are discovered by others. As they travel, they each have a fun adventure and discover love.

Under One Sky

When Love Collides

Don't miss out!

Visit the website below and you can sign up to receive emails whenever Zoe Matthews publishes a new book. There's no charge and no obligation.

https://books2read.com/r/B-A-NKT-VDEG

BOOKS 2 READ

Connecting independent readers to independent writers.

Made in the USA
Monee, IL
28 September 2021

78941442R00055